KING
OF THE
CREEPS

Steven Banks

Alfred A. Knopf
New York

THIS IS A BORZOI BOOK PUBLISHED BY ALFRED A. KNOPF

Published in the United States by Alfred A. Knopf, an imprint of Random House Children's Books, a division of Random House, Inc., New York.

KNOPF, BORZOI BOOKS, and the colophon are registered trademarks of Random House, Inc.

www.randomhouse.com/teens

Educators and librarians, for a variety of teaching tools, visit us at
www.randomhouse.com/teachers

Library of Congress Cataloging-in-Publication Data
Banks, Steven.
King of the creeps / Steven Banks. — 1st ed.
p. cm.
SUMMARY: When a nerdy, unpopular high school senior notices his resemblance to Bob Dylan, he leaves home for Greenwich Village, in 1963, to become a folk singer.
ISBN-13: 978-0-375-832918 (trade) — ISBN-13: 978-0-375-932915 (lib. bdg.)
ISBN 0-375-83291-2 (trade) — ISBN 0-375-93291-7 (lib. bdg.)
[1. Folk music—Fiction. 2. Singers—Fiction. 3. Self-confidence—Fiction. 4. New York (N.Y.)—History—20th century—Fiction. 5. Humorous stories.] I. Title.
PZ7.B22637Ki 2006
[Fic]—dc22
2005033270

Printed in the United States of America
10 9 8 7 6 5 4 3 2 1
First Edition

To my favorite teacher, Annette

*Don't judge a book
by its cover.*

THE WORST DAY OF MY LIFE

It all began the day I was going to jump off the George Washington Bridge.

I had a good reason. I was seventeen years old. At seventeen everybody has at least one reason. I had about a hundred and forty.

I was short.

I was skinny.

I had frizzy hair.

I had a big nose.

I was a creep.

How much worse could it get?

Much worse. I had to get glasses. The day this all started I went to the optometrist for my first pair of glasses. The doctor was this big smiley guy, and when he put the glasses on me for the first time he said, "Now, I bet that's an improvement!"

What did he think he was doing? Entering me in the 1963 Creep of the Year contest? Did he think glasses would improve my chances of winning?

As I was leaving, the doctor was still smiling, and he patted me on the shoulder and said, "Tommy, you're going to love your new glasses."

For a doctor, he was pretty stupid. Nobody loved their glasses. I hated mine. They were the ugliest glasses in the world. Big, black, thick ones that made me look worse than before. But, I have to admit, I could see a lot better.

My mother had this crazy idea that I looked like President Kennedy. *She* was the one who needed glasses. Trust me; I don't look like President Kennedy. Once I was getting my hair cut and I asked the barber to give me a haircut like Kennedy because I heard these girls say they thought he was a handsome guy. The barber laughed for about fifteen minutes and then he gave me the same old haircut I always got.

Some people thought I looked like this weird guy on TV who showed cartoons every afternoon. His name was Silly Sammy and people used to call me that all the time.

"Hey! Silly Sammy! Do something with your banana!"

Silly Sammy was always doing stupid stuff with a banana. His show was brought to you by the people that made Delepeña bananas and so he always had a big pile of bananas on his desk. Once, when I was a kid and I still watched the show, he made a hat out of bananas, so I tried to do it and I wrecked all the bananas my mom had just bought. She didn't get very mad, but my father did.

I hate to admit it, but I do sort of look like Silly Sammy. We're both short and skinny and have funny hair and a big nose. The only thing I don't have that would make me look worse is freckles. I figured I'd probably get them someday. I'd wake up and all of a sudden I'd have freckles.

The only thing I knew I was safe from getting was braces. My father would never pay for them. One good thing about getting glasses was that I was missing speech class. I hated speech class. Getting up in front of the class and talking was just horrible. Everybody stared at you and I always made about a million mistakes. The only other good thing about getting glasses was that I wouldn't look like Silly Sammy anymore because he didn't wear glasses.

But, getting back to being a creep, the worst thing about being a creep is that girls don't go out with creeps.

EVER.

The only kind of girls that go out with creeps are dogs. And who wanted to go out with a dog? I mean, even creeps have standards. So, I was a creep and I had standards, and I had no experience with any kind of girl.

None.

I had never *dated* a girl.

I had never *kissed* a girl.

I had never even *held hands* with a girl.

I tried to hold hands with a girl once. She was sitting next

3

to me at this dumb football game my father made me go to. I hate football. I'm really lousy at sports, especially football and basketball and track and baseball.

Anyway, when he made me go to this stupid football game I was really bored until this girl sat down next to me. She was really short. I thought for a minute she might even be a midget or something, but I didn't care because she was really cute and she smelled great and when she sat down she said, "Hi." Now normally I would just say hi and then never say anything else because everything I would think of to say would sound stupid. But then she said, "I hate football," and I said, "So do I," and we just started talking. She was with her uncle, who watched the whole game through his binoculars. He never let her use them once. I couldn't believe it. If I ever took someone to a football game, which I wouldn't because I hate football, I'd at least share my binoculars with them. Her name was Ellen and every once in a while she would start biting her fingernails. Usually this would bug me, but I didn't care because she was pretty and she was talking to me. She kept biting her fingernails through the whole game, and it was a really long and boring game.

I started joking around and I kept grabbing her hand and pulling her fingers out of her mouth and saying, "Stop biting your nails, miss!" And then she'd laugh and then I'd let go of her hand real fast so she wouldn't think I was trying to hold her hand, which is exactly what I was trying to do. My plan was to eventually say, "I'm just gonna have to hold on to this hand so you don't bite your fingers off." Then I wouldn't let go of her hand, so I would actually be holding her hand. But, of course,

I didn't do it because I thought she'd hit me or something. So I just looked at the boring football game and never held her hand. She was really pretty. She had short blond hair and freckles. Freckles looked good on her because she didn't have a million of them. She kind of looked like that actress Sandra Dee, who was in those Gidget movies about all those surfers. I figured she was just being nice to me because she was bored with the football game. She probably had some big handsome boyfriend at her school. Pretty girls only went out with handsome guys or sports guys and it didn't even matter if the guys were stupid or jerks. Those guys just went up to girls and asked them out and the girls went out with them. I'm not a Poindexter genius type, but I'm a lot smarter than those big dumb guys, and if I went out with a girl, I'd be *really* nice to her.

It wasn't that I didn't try to ask girls out. I did. Sort of.

The week before I got my stupid glasses I made a list of nine different girls that wouldn't be completely horrible to ask to this big school dance they have every Thanksgiving called the Tom Turkey Dance. I was going to use the phone in my parents' bedroom so nobody would hear me, and I wrote down exactly what I was going to say. I called the first girl and some bratty little kid answered the phone and I chickened out and hung up.

I had given up on the whole Tom Turkey Dance until my mom brought it up when she and my father were driving me to the optometrist to get my glasses. My father came along to make sure the doctor didn't gyp him. They picked me up from school at lunchtime and we had to go clear down to East Brunswick because somebody had told my father that the doctor there had the cheapest prices.

5

Anyway, my father was driving, my mom was next to him, and I was in the backseat. We drove by this sign with a big turkey wearing a Pilgrim hat, and she turned around to me in the backseat and gave me this smile and said, "Honey, isn't the Tom Turkey Dance coming up soon?"

"I guess so," I said.

"Are you going to go?"

I slouched down in the backseat. "I dunno."

"Have you asked anybody?"

"Not yet."

"Are you going to?"

I slouched down farther. "I dunno. Maybe."

My father looked at me in the rearview mirror. "Sit up."

I sat up and my mom turned back around in her seat. "Well, Tommy, don't wait too long. Girls don't like to be asked at the last minute."

"I won't," I said. Of course, I was lying. I wasn't going to ask anyone.

"Good," said my mom. "I bet there's some very nice girl just waiting for you to call her."

She always says stuff like that. She's always being nice and she's always in a good mood, which isn't the easiest thing in the world being married to my father, who was usually in a bad mood. Sometimes I wondered why she married him. There are pictures of her when she was really young and she used to be pretty. I mean, I know she's my mom and everything, but she was pretty. My father was just sort of normal-looking.

I didn't want to keep talking about the Tom Turkey Dance,

so I leaned forward, reached across the front seat, and turned on the radio. I tried to tune in a station but it was all static since the radio hadn't worked for about a hundred years.

My mom sighed and said, "Harold, when are you going to get this radio fixed?"

Without taking his eyes off the road, my father slammed his hand against the dashboard.

BAM!

My mom jumped about ten feet out of her seat. The radio came in loud and clear.

My father smiled. "It's fixed."

That's how he fixed things, by hitting them. He was hitting things all the time. Radios, TVs, toasters, refrigerators, record players.

My mother was not giving up on this Tom Turkey Dance. "Why don't you ask Carol Pace?"

My mother was crazy. Carol Pace was this girl at school who every single guy was in love with. She wouldn't go out with me if I paid her a million dollars.

"She has a boyfriend," I said.

"Well, what about that girl—"

"I heard a good one yesterday," said my father. He was always interrupting my mom. I was kind of glad, because as much as I hated his jokes, it was better than talking about the Tom Turkey Dance. "What do you call it when the Kennedy family goes swimming in the ocean?"

My mom and I always pretended that we liked my father's jokes. He got a big kick out of telling them. But right then I was trying to find a radio station that was playing some music and my mom was probably thinking of some other girl who would never go out with me and so we both forgot to answer him.

"Hey! I'm telling a joke here!" he shouted. "What do you call it when the Kennedy family goes swimming in the ocean?"

My mom pretended to get all excited. "I don't know, Harold, what?"

My father sat up straight and then said the punch line real loud, like he was on TV or something. "A Bay of Pigs!"

I didn't think it was a very funny joke, but I laughed so he wouldn't think I didn't get it. My mother laughed a little bit, but she waited too long to do it.

My father hated it when she did that. "Louise, you didn't get it, did you? Don't laugh at something unless you know why you're laughing! The Bay of Pigs was the invasion of Cuba that Kennedy botched. The Kennedys are all pigs, so when they go swimming . . . Bay of Pigs!"

My mother did a really fake laugh.

I finally found some music on the radio. It was this guy playing a guitar and a harmonica and he sounded like an old guy singing, but you could tell he was young.

> *How many years can a mountain exist,*
> *Before it's washed to the sea?*
> *Yes, 'n' how many years can some people exist,*
> *Before they're allowed to be free?*

My father had a fit. "What the hell is that?"

*Yes, 'n' how many times can a man turn his
    head,*
Pretending he just doesn't see?

My father started making all these faces. "This moron is giving me a headache!"

The answer, my friend, is blowin' in the wind,
The answer is blowin' in the wind.

"Who is this idiot?" My father was getting real worked up. He started talking to the radio. He does this a lot. "I'll tell you what the answer is. The answer is, You're a moron! You're an idiot singing a stupid song! What is this? This isn't music!"

I said, "I think he's a folksinger."

"In no way, shape, or form is that guy a singer," said my father. "Change it!"

I changed the radio to another station, where they were playing "Ramblin' Rose" by Nat King Cole.

My father smiled. "Now, *that* is a singer. Mr. Nat King Cole. That's a voice!"

My mom said, "Oh, I just love him. He has such a wonderful voice."

My father got real serious. "You know why, don't you? It's because he has a big nose."

"Oh, Harold, that's ridiculous."

"It's the truth! I didn't make this up. Everything resonates in there. It's like a little echo chamber. Think of it: Nat King

Cole, Harry Belafonte, Ray Charles, they all got big, wide noses and that's why they sound so good."

My mother sighed. She sighed all the time. "Harold, that just isn't true. I can't believe you would say that."

"Now, wait a minute, Louise, I'm not being prejudiced. It's not just negroes. Remember that Jewish girl we saw on *The Ed Sullivan Show*? With the nose? She looked like an anteater? Great voice! Big nose equals big voice."

Now even I knew this was crazy, because I had a big nose and I didn't have a great voice. I mean, I wasn't lousy; I used to sing in school choirs and stuff, but I wasn't like a professional singer. But you couldn't argue with my father. So no one ever did, except my mom.

"Okay, Harold. What about Frank Sinatra?" asked my mom. "He doesn't have a big nose."

My father didn't say anything for a while. Frank Sinatra was his favorite singer. He loved him. He had about a million of his albums and played them all the time. Finally he said, "Sinatra is different."

My mother sighed again, which really drove my father crazy. "Louise, stop sighing all the time!"

My mom changed the subject. "You know, we should try to go see *The Ed Sullivan Show* sometime. It's so close to us. Here we are in New Jersey, right across the river from New York City, and we've never been."

My father snorted. "Why pay for something you can see on TV for free?"

"But, Harold, Jane Martin got tickets last year and they were free."

We watched *The Ed Sullivan Show* every single Sunday night. Everybody watched it. It was a pretty good show. They always had on really famous singers and movie stars and comedians and jugglers and dog acts and magicians and people singing opera and acrobats and dancers and every kind of act you could think of. It was a good show because if you didn't like the act that was on, there was always another one coming up right away that you probably would like.

The song ended and the DJ said, "That was Nat King Cole, one of the greatest singers of all time."

My father smiled. "I rest my case!"

Then the DJ said, "And now for something different, here's folksinger Bob Dylan with his version of *Blowin' in the Wind.*"

It was the same guy as before with the weird voice.

My father almost ran off the road. "This moron must be paying somebody to be on the radio! Turn it off!"

My mom turned it off as fast as she could.

We *finally* got to the optometrist's and I got my stupid glasses and the doctor was all smiley and my father made sure he wasn't getting gypped. Then we had to drop my father off at work, then my mom would take me back to school, which was really dumb because I only had one more class, then my mom would go home and do whatever it was she did during the day.

We got back in the car and I turned on the radio. A record was playing, but then the announcer stopped it in the middle and said, "This just in from Texas . . . ," and then the radio got all staticky again and my father turned it off. I started fooling around with my glasses and my father sighed and said, "Tommy, stop playing with your glasses."

My mom looked at her watch. "I hope you're not missing anything important at school."

"Just lunch and speech class," I said.

"Speech class?" My father shook his head. "That'll do you a lot of good. You gonna make speeches for a living?"

My mom turned around and looked at me and smiled. "Well, someday he may have to get up in front of a lot of people and say something important."

My father shook his head. "Yeah, right, and I'm gonna sing on *The Ed Sullivan Show*."

We dropped my father off at his job. He worked at the Harlan Machine Company. It was a big factory and he was in charge of the screw machines, which make parts for other machines. I didn't like to tell people what he did because they always made really dumb dirty jokes.

Anyway, he got out of the car and then he pointed his finger at me and looked at me really serious.

"Son?"

"Yes, sir?"

"Anybody calls you four-eyes, you beat the crap out of 'em."

"Yes, sir," I said, and threw in a halfhearted nod. My father was crazy. How could he possibly think I could ever beat up anybody with my skinny arms? The last fight I was in had been seven years ago, when I was ten years old. I lost to this girl named Tracy Sinclair, who was only eight, but she was about three times bigger than me.

My father walked into his office building and I got in the

front seat and my mom drove. She wasn't giving up on this Tom Turkey Dance.

"Did you know that there's a new girl who moved in next to the Graysons? Why not ask her?"

"Mom, why waste the time? I know what she's gonna say."

"No, you don't."

"Yes, I do. She'll say no, like every other girl."

"What about Tracy Sinclair?"

I was not going to ask a girl who had beaten me up.

"No."

"What about that nice girl, Kelly Pittson? I bet she'd go out with you."

"No, she wouldn't."

"How do you know?"

"Because nobody wants to go out with a creep."

My mother almost crashed the car after I said that.

"Thomas Johnson! Don't you *ever* say that!"

"Mom, it's the truth. Look at me. I'm short!"

"You're still growing."

"I'm skinny."

"You're just slim."

"I have funny hair."

"You do not have funny hair!"

"I have a big nose."

"You have a very nice nose!"

"And now I have to wear these stupid glasses!"

"There's nothing wrong with wearing glasses."

"Mom, face it, I'm a creep."

She didn't say anything for a while. I could tell she was

trying to think of something to say that would make me feel better. We drove about a block and then she started talking again.

"The most popular boy at my high school was a boy named Albert Eaves, and he didn't look like a movie star. But he was so nice and so funny that everybody was crazy about him. Now, you have a very nice personality and a good sense of humor. Girls like boys with nice personalities. They want to laugh and have fun. Make a girl laugh and she'll go out with you."

"Did you go out with that guy?" I asked.

My mom looked out the window for a second. "Yes. I did."

I knew she was lying. She'd never gone out with that Albert Eaves guy. She just said she did to make me feel better. And actually that started to make me feel worse. Then I started to think that there probably hadn't even been a guy named Albert Eaves in the first place. She'd made him up so her creepy son wouldn't feel like a creep.

We finally pulled up in front of the school and my mom stopped the car. I think she could tell I hadn't bought her Albert Eaves story. I started to get out and she grabbed my hand. She started to speak in this really quiet voice that she only used when she was really mad or about to cry. "Tommy, you are what is known as a late bloomer. You will grow into your looks and be a very handsome man."

"Well, right now I'm a very ugly kid."

I really wished I hadn't said that, because my mom kind of yelled at me. "You are not ugly! Don't you ever say that! Now get going, you're late."

I got out of the car and watched her drive away. She had

one hand on the steering wheel and she was wiping her eyes with the other one. I watched her drive all the way down the street and turn the corner.

I turned around and looked up at Rutherford B. Hayes High School.

There were three hundred and forty-seven girls in that building.

All I wanted was one.

And all of a sudden one was walking out of the front door, heading right toward me.

RAY GILLETTE'S LOUSY KNOT

It was Janie Workman. She was this gorgeous girl, not stuck-up at all, even though she was really smart and hung around with the kids who were stuck-up and thought they were hotshots and everybody else was beneath them. They thought they ran the school and all the teachers thought they were really nice and would grow up to be fine, upstanding members of the community. I thought they were jerks. But, to be honest, I'd rather be a stuck-up jerk than a creep, just so I could hang around with Janie Workman. She had this great smile and beautiful blue eyes and perfect skin, and I know it sounds weird, but she always looked really clean, like she'd just taken a shower and washed her hair. Once I stood behind her when she was getting a drink at the drinking fountain, and I got kind of close to her and I could smell her perfume or shampoo. I thought I was going to have a heart attack. I didn't know people could smell that good.

Anyway, Janie came out of the school and sat down on one of the ugly cement benches they have in front near the flagpole. The benches have these little plaques with the names of old, dead people who went to the school a hundred years ago. Janie looked like she had just gotten an F on a test or they'd kicked her out of school. I knew that hadn't happened because she was the smartest girl in the senior class. But she looked really serious and she never looked serious, she was always happy and smiling. So, here's where I made one of my all-time stupidest moves. I took my mother's advice about making a girl laugh. I walked over to Janie and said, "Hi. I heard a good joke. You wanna hear it?"

I was going to tell a joke I had heard this comedian tell on *The Ed Sullivan Show* about a moose. He was a short, skinny, nervous little guy with glasses and a big nose. I looked like him, too. Anyway, it was a really good joke, but standing there that close to Janie I got all nervous and couldn't remember how it started. She was just staring at me with those beautiful blue eyes and I had to say something.

"What do you call it when the Kennedy family goes swimming in the ocean?"

She looked at me like I'd just run over her dog.

I actually said the punch line really loud, the way my father does. I hate it when he does that, but I did it anyway. I practically shouted out, "A Bay of Pigs!"

I couldn't believe what happened next.

Janie Workman, the prettiest and smartest and nicest girl in the senior class, stood up and slapped me.

WHAM!

My new glasses flew off my head and went flying through the air. Don't ever let anybody tell you that girls aren't strong or they can't hurt you. It *really* hurt. It hurt so bad I had to blink my eyes really fast so I wouldn't start crying. Can you imagine crying in front of a girl? Especially one like Janie Workman? It wasn't like in the movies where guys beat each other up for an hour and nobody cries or yells or anything. I couldn't believe it; she was just a girl and not really strong and she had a little hand, but I would not want to be hit by her again for a million bucks. The whole left side of my face was burning. Meanwhile, *Janie* started crying. It was horrible.

She looked at me and said, "I pity you."

Then she walked away and I heard a crunching noise. She had stepped right on my new glasses. I don't think she did it on purpose, but I don't think she was sorry she did.

And then it got worse.

I forgot to tell you something. It sort of puts the final nail in the creep coffin. Last year, when I was a junior, I was the school flag monitor. *Nobody* wanted to be flag monitor. You had to be the first person at school in the morning and you had to stand in front of everybody, waiting for school to start. Then you had to raise the flag while this kid named Jerry Stockdale played "The Star-Spangled Banner" on the trumpet. He was a lousy trumpet player, but he was the only kid who would do it so they had to use him. You'd think he would get better playing the same song every single day, but he never did.

Anyway, this year the flag monitor was Ray Gillette. He was a mess. A royal mess. He made me look like Cary Grant or that guy who plays James Bond or any handsome movie star you can think of. Ray *always* blew it. He never tied the rope tight enough. When I was flag monitor I always tied a really tight knot. Ray couldn't tie a knot if his life depended on it. So, I wasn't completely surprised when, after Janie walked away, I looked up and saw that the flag was halfway down the pole. Way to go, Ray, I thought.

I went over and untied Ray's crummy knot. I started to raise the flag up to the top of the pole. The wind was blowing a little bit and the flag looked kind of neat, and I don't know why, but I felt kind of patriotic. Here I was raising the Stars and Stripes over my school in a free country. Not like Russia. They'd probably shoot you if you were late for school. And you'd probably have to wait years to get a pair of glasses. And if you were a creep? Forget it, they'd probably send you to Siberia, which was supposed to be the worst prison in the world. I tied a really good, tight knot, and I looked up at the flag and I almost kind of felt like saluting, but I didn't want to be a complete jerk. I could just imagine the whole school seeing me standing out there by myself saluting the flag. I was smiling this dopey kind of smile and looking up at the flag blowing around, so I didn't see Mr. Liotta, the vice principal, come running out of the school like the place was on fire.

"Johnson!" he yelled.

He really scared me. He was mad. And he wasn't the only person who was mad. I looked behind him toward the school and it seemed like every single class was standing at their windows banging on the glass and yelling. They were going nuts.

Mr. Liotta grabbed me by my collar. He was about two inches from my face, yelling at me. "What do you think you're doing, Johnson?"

He had *really* bad halitosis, so I turned my head away so I wouldn't have to smell his stinky breath.

"Look at me when I'm talking to you, Johnson!"

I turned to look back at him but held my breath so I wouldn't have to smell his bad breath.

"What do you think you're doing, Johnson?"

"I . . . I was raising the flag. It slipped."

He shook me really hard again. "It didn't slip, Johnson! The flag is at half-mast! President Kennedy was assassinated!"

When he said it I couldn't believe it. It felt like I was on that TV show *The Twilight Zone* and I was an astronaut who had just come back from a space mission and they were telling me all this crazy stuff that had happened while I was gone. It was so weird to think that somebody had shot Kennedy. I knew there were people who didn't like him and thought he was a lousy president, but I didn't think anybody hated him so much that they would kill him. That was crazy. I mean, my parents were Republicans and my father hated President Kennedy, but it was different.

I asked my father once why he hated him so much. He gave me this big, long answer about how Kennedy was a rich, spoiled

Catholic whose father had bought him the presidency with all the money he had made bootlegging and how he was spending too much money on the space program when he should have been fighting communism. And my father didn't just hate President Kennedy; he hated the whole family. He hated President Kennedy's father and his brothers, Bobby and Teddy. He hated his wife, Jackie Kennedy, because he thought she was a stuck-up snob. He even hated the two little kids, John-John and Caroline. Why would you hate two little kids? My father was crazy.

Mr. Liotta *loved* President Kennedy. He was always talking about how great the president was and how he wished he could quit being a vice principal and go join the Peace Corps and help people in Africa. I didn't know what was stopping him.

Anyway, he was really mad at me for raising the flag. He was yelling at me and then all of a sudden he started crying. I'd never seen a man cry, especially that close up to me. I'd never seen my father cry, even when my grandpa died. I don't think my father had ever cried in his whole life, except when he was a baby. Mr. Liotta was *really* crying. It was kind of scary. He was wiping his eyes and his face was all red and then snot started coming out of his nose, which made me want to barf. But I guess if I loved President Kennedy as much as he did I'd be bawling, too.

I felt bad about Kennedy being shot, but I have to admit I felt worse about my new glasses being broken and the whole school yelling at me and Janie Workman slapping me and the fact that I was a creep.

It was the worst day of my life.

So, after I lowered the flag to half-mast again, and Mr. Liotta went back inside, I decided to go to the George Washington Bridge and jump off. It wasn't like when you're a kid and you say you're going to run away from home and you only go about a block and you get tired and hungry and you turn around. I was really going to do it.

JEANNIE AND CONNIE

The George Washington Bridge was a pretty high bridge. I used to spit off it when I was a kid and it took about four and a half seconds until the spit hit the water. I used to pretend my spit was a bomb and I was dropping bombs on Russian submarines.

I started walking toward the bridge, through downtown, and I went by Grayson's Music store. I don't know why I did it, but for some weird reason, I stopped and looked at my reflection in Grayson's window. I looked at myself: my big nose, my short, skinny body, and my frizzy hair. Then I looked at the stuff they had in the window. They had records and those shiny pictures of famous singers. All the handsome guys that the girls went for like Elvis Presley, Rick Nelson, Jack Jones, Andy Williams, and Robert Goulet. They were dressed up in suits or tuxedos and looking either really happy or really serious. They looked like they were about to go to a big Hollywood party or a movie premiere or fly to Las Vegas or go all the way with some beautiful actress or model.

I was definitely not going to do any of those things. So I was about to go to the George Washington Bridge, and I would have if I hadn't looked down and seen something else in the corner of the window.

It was a record album with a yellow sign above it that said ON SALE $1.98. On the cover of the album was a picture of a guy and girl walking down the middle of the street. It looked like it was in New York City. There were old buildings on either side with fire escapes and there was some snow in the street. The guy had his hands in his front pockets and she was holding on to his arm and kind of hugging him. The girl was really pretty. She looked a little bit like Janie Workman. She had long, light brown hair hanging down past her shoulders. You could tell just from looking at her that she smelled really nice. She was smiling and happy, like the guy had just told her a really funny story or a joke or something. You could tell that she was madly in love with this guy, and she was holding on to him like she'd never let him go. She looked like she was the happiest girl in the world.

And then I looked at the guy.

He was short.

He was skinny.

His hair was frizzy.

He kind of had a big nose.

HE WAS A CREEP!

I leaned in closer to the window to get a better look, and the glass got all fogged up, so I wiped it clear with my sleeve. The guy on the cover looked kind of like a hobo. He was wearing boots and blue jeans and he had on this dirty, beat-up, old brown jacket with the collar turned up.

I got all excited because the guy looked just like me and there he was with a beautiful girl. Then I thought, Wait a minute, that girl is just some model they hired for the picture. She's probably real stuck-up and hated having to stand next to a creepy little guy. No good-looking girl would go for him. Who were they trying to kid?

It was just a stupid picture on a stupid record.

I turned away and was about to leave when I heard two girls laughing. Usually I get excited when I hear that, but right then it made me want to barf. They were coming around the corner and I didn't want anybody to see me. I couldn't run away, so I hid behind these two big mailboxes.

I peeked around and saw it was two girls from my school, Jeannie Thomas and Connie Brand. They were really pretty. Jeannie was a blond and Connie was a brunette and they were always together. They kind of looked like Betty and Veronica in the *Archie* comics and some people even called them that. The school must have let everybody out a little bit early because President Kennedy got killed. Anyway, when they passed Grayson's Music, Jeannie grabbed Connie's arm and yanked her over to the window.

"Oh my God! Connie! Look! There's that Bob Dylan album I was telling you about!"

They were talking about the album I had just seen. I hadn't even looked to see what the album was called. Bob Dylan was the guy I had heard on the radio that morning, the folksinger with the weird voice that my father hated.

Jeannie was having a cow. She was pressing her face so close to the window, it looked like she was going to kiss it. She was right where my face had been. If she'd known, she probably would have barfed. Connie put her face right up against the window, too, and let out a big sigh. "He is so . . . real."

"And he's so cute," said Jeannie. "Look at those eyes."

Connie started playing with her hair so it would puff up higher. She and Jeannie both had those beehive hairdos that went way up.

"Didja know he really was an orphan?" asked Connie.

Jeannie started playing with her hair to make it go higher than Connie's. "Everybody knows that. And he still is an orphan. You don't stop being an orphan."

Connie whispered real dramatically, "It's so sad."

Jeannie was smiling. I guess she wasn't as sad about this guy being an orphan. "I wish my parents would adopt him."

Connie shook her head. "No, you don't. Then he couldn't be your boyfriend. It'd be against the law."

Jeannie made that noise with her tongue that drives my father crazy. "I don't think so, Miss No Brain. That's only if he's your *real* brother, not your *adopted* brother."

Connie started to get mad. "Well, my uncle's a lawyer and I'm gonna ask him."

Jeannie stopped playing with her hair, because it was higher than Connie's. "Well, I wouldn't care if it was against the law. I'd tuck him into bed every single night and give him a nice, long good-night kiss!"

My knees were getting sore, crouching behind the mailboxes. I wanted to change positions, but I couldn't move because they might hear me. If they knew I was spying on them, they'd probably kill me. Or have their boyfriends do it. Jeannie went with a guy named Tim Hatcher, who was a pole-vaulter on the track team. He had big Popeye arms. Girls love stuff like that.

Connie went with a guy named Doug McGrath, who really did look like President Kennedy. He had a really tough car, too. It was a red Corvette Sting Ray. He was always laying rubber in front of the school and showing off. Everybody said that's why Connie went with him, because he had the toughest car. They also said that the only reason he went with Connie was because she had the biggest boobs of any girl at school. They were *huge*. And it was weird, because up until eighth grade Connie was flat as a pancake, but then all of a sudden she was stacked. She could have been a *Playboy* model if she wanted. She was a real sexpot. Guys used to climb up on a fence near the gym to watch her run around the track during P.E. I never did it. But, to be honest, that's because I never had P.E. when she did. I probably would have.

Jeannie reached in her purse and pulled out a pack of cigarettes. I couldn't believe it. She was the last girl you would think would smoke. "Y'know, Connie, Bob Dylan really cares about stuff, like negroes and the A-bomb." It took her three matches to light her cigarette.

Connie started to make this funny noise, like she had something stuck between her two front teeth. "Y'know, I bet he writes a song about JFK getting shot."

"Yeah, I bet he does," said Jeannie. "Did you see on TV? Jackie was still wearing that dress with the bloodstains on it!"

Connie made a face. "That was disgusting! If my husband got shot and I got blood on my dress, I would *never* do that! Yuck!"

"I wonder if she'll ever get married again," said Jeannie, and then she started coughing. She wasn't really smoking, she was faking it. She blew the smoke right out, she didn't inhale it like you're supposed to. I tried to smoke once, when I was ten, with this kid named Billy Barkley. We stole two of his grandfather's cigarettes. It tasted horrible. I kept coughing and I was really bad at it. Billy was pretty good at it, but he had done it before. His grandfather found out that we stole the cigarettes and he spanked Billy, right in front of me. He even pulled down Billy's pants *and* underpants to do it. Billy said he'd pound me if I ever told anybody. He dropped out of school in the tenth grade. I see him every once in a while downtown and he's always smoking.

"I bet Jackie Kennedy becomes a nun," said Connie.

"Can you be a nun if you have kids?" asked Jeannie in between coughs.

Connie shrugged. "Beats me."

"And what would she do with her kids if she was a nun? Who would take care of them?"

"I don't know! I'm not the pope!"

Connie took Jeannie's cigarette and she didn't smoke it right, either, but at least she didn't cough. "I feel sorry for her."

"Me too. But what is with her voice? She's always whispering."

"She sounds like Marilyn Monroe used to talk."

"Yeah. But she's not as pretty as Marilyn Monroe was. To tell the truth, I don't think she's that pretty at all. She's like a fish, with those big eyes way over on either side of her face. You know who looks like her? Katie Mott."

"Who?" asked Connie.

"You know, the sophomore who thinks she's a ballerina. She was in the talent show last year . . ." All of a sudden Jeannie grabbed Connie and screamed, "Oh my God! I have got the best idea!" She was so excited she was jumping around like she had to go to the bathroom. "We should do a song about President Kennedy for the school talent show! You can play the guitar and I'll sing!"

Connie looked worried. "I haven't played the guitar since sixth grade. Anyway, my mother gave it away to my cousin."

"We could buy one!" said Jeannie.

"I'm not going to waste my money on a stupid guitar," said Connie. "They cost a fortune."

"No, they don't! My brother bought one in New York at this place called Max's in Greenwich Village and it was really cheap."

"Does your brother ever ask about me?"

"No. What should we wear for the talent show?"

"Doesn't he like me?"

"He's a big jerk." Jeannie was looking at herself in Grayson's window. "I have this *gorgeous* new blouse I could wear with my black capris, but I need new shoes."

"Why doesn't your brother like me?"

Jeannie was kind of getting mad. "I don't know! Forget about my brother, we gotta write a song for the talent show."

"What kind of song?"

"Just a song about President Kennedy, about how sad we feel that he died and all that."

"Jeannie, we don't know how to write a song!"

"How hard can it be? You just write a poem and then add some music. We'll just use the music from some old folk song and write our own words."

"What kind of words?"

"Like . . . uh." Jeannie was thinking. She closed her eyes and was kind of talking to herself and then she jumped up and down again. "I got it! I got it!" Then she started singing:

> *I felt so sad when President Kennedy died,*
> *I felt so sad that I sat down and cried.*

"That's really good." Connie was impressed. "I bet we could win!"

"I *know* we could win!"

"We'll get our picture in the yearbook!"

They both started jumping around like they had to go to the bathroom. Then all of a sudden Connie stopped jumping and grabbed Jeannie. "Wait a minute. Do you think we could beat that blind girl who plays the piano?"

Jeannie sighed. "Oh, shit!"

I couldn't *believe* that Jeannie Thomas said "shit."

"I forgot about her. She always wins! It's not fair. They just give it to her because she's blind."

"I know," said Connie. "And she gets her picture in the yearbook and she can't even see it! I mean, what's the point?"

"Yeah. You're right. The talent show is stupid anyway. Just a bunch of people showing off. Besides, I'd rather go *out* with a folksinger than *be* one."

"Yeah, me too."

Jeannie looked back at the album cover and tried to blow a smoke ring. "How'd you like to be that girl Dylan's with?"

"Lucky puppy!" squealed Connie.

"I read that's his real girlfriend."

"You know, she looks like Judy Swanson from gym class."

Jeannie frowned. "Sort of. Hey, did you know Judy wears falsies?"

"You lie!"

"I saw her putting them in! She made me swear I wouldn't tell anybody."

Okay. First, I couldn't believe that Judy Swanson wore falsies. But more important, I couldn't believe that girl on the album cover wasn't a model. She was actually that creepy guy's real girlfriend.

Jeannie and Connie both stared at the picture for a while.

"You know, she's not that pretty," said Connie.

"I know," said Jeannie.

"You're *a lot* prettier."

"I know. So are you."

This wasn't exactly true. Jeannie and Connie and the girl on the album cover were *all* pretty. I would have been happy with any of them.

"Wouldn't you just die to be Dylan's girlfriend?" asked Connie

"Yeah. I'd give anything to be in her shoes."

"I bet she wears great shoes! He probably takes her shopping and she gets anything she wants."

Connie tried to light another cigarette but gave up. "It would be so cool to go to Greenwich Village and meet Dylan and get his autograph."

"I'd want more than just a stupid old autograph."

"What do you mean?"

Jeannie looked around and then she whispered, but I could hear her because I was so close. "If Bob Dylan asked me to, I'd go all the way with him."

Connie's jaw dropped about ten feet. "Jeannie Thomas!"

"I would."

"Would not!"

"Would too."

"You lie like a rug!"

"I'd like to do it on a rug, in front of a fireplace, with some wine and candles."

Connie was having a coronary. "Jeannie Thomas, you are my best friend, but you are going to go to hell."

Jeannie smiled this really sexy smile. "He'd be worth it."

I didn't jump off the George Washington Bridge.

I decided to become a folksinger.

FREDDIE THE FREELOADER

If I took every Charles Atlas muscle-building course available, if I exercised twenty-four hours a day for the rest of my life, I'd never be a big football player guy. And I'd never be a handsome guy unless I had a million dollars' worth of plastic surgery.

But a folksinger? This was something I could be.

I mean, there was Jeannie Thomas, a really pretty girl, saying she'd go all the way with a short, skinny, frizzy-haired, big-nosed creep. I know I wasn't famous and couldn't play the guitar or write songs and my picture wasn't on a record album, but at least I had the look. It was a start. Like Jeannie Thomas said, how hard could it be?

All I needed were some old clothes and a guitar. It wouldn't be long before I'd have a pretty girl with long hair walking down the street with me, laughing at my jokes, holding on to my arm and never letting go.

I wanted to go into Manhattan right then and buy one of those cheap guitars at that place that Jeannie had talked about. But I knew I couldn't because I had to get home. When I got there, my mom was watching the news about President Kennedy on TV. She was pretty upset. I watched for a little while, but to be honest it was kind of boring because they just kept showing the same thing over and over. I was just about to go upstairs when we heard my father get dropped off from work. Mr. Platt, this guy who works at the same place, always drives him home. He was whistling when he came in the door and he didn't notice I wasn't wearing my glasses.

"Oh, Harold," said my mom. "Isn't it just awful?"

He didn't say anything. He just sat down on the sofa. On the TV they were showing pictures of Kennedy playing with his kids. My mom was shaking her head. "He was so young."

"Tom, change the channel," said my father.

I got up and changed the channel on the TV and there was more stuff about the president. I changed channels again. All seven channels had something about President Kennedy. One of the channels was just showing pictures of him and playing that kind of classical music they make you listen to in elementary school when it rains and you can't play outside.

My father shook his head. "Oh, brother."

"Harold, I know you didn't like him, but nevertheless, he was our president and he didn't deserve to be killed."

Then they showed Jackie Kennedy walking around in her dress with the blood on it. Jeannie Thomas was crazy; she didn't look like a fish, she was pretty. She looked like the saddest woman in the world. My mom shook her head and said, "I feel so sorry for that poor, poor woman."

"What's for dinner?" asked my father.

I had to wait a whole week before I could go buy the guitar. I wanted to go the next day, on Saturday, but my father made me do all this stupid stuff around the house. Because of Kennedy getting killed everything was kind of crazy. All the regular TV shows went off the air and all they showed was stuff about him all weekend. Then Lee Harvey Oswald, the guy who shot Kennedy, *he* got shot right on TV. I couldn't believe it. That was really weird. I know I shouldn't say it, but I have to admit I thought it was kind of cool. It wasn't like in the movies at all. There wasn't any blood or anything. He just kind of grabbed his stomach and his face got all screwed up. But since he killed the president I guess it wasn't so bad that he got shot.

On Monday at school they made us watch President Kennedy's funeral on TV. I didn't mind. It was during P.E., and watching a funeral, even though it was really long and kind of boring, was better than getting clobbered playing football. A lot of the girls cried, but I think some of them were faking it just so people would pay attention to them. Jeannie Thomas and Connie Brand were crying buckets. Janie Workman, the girl who slapped me and broke my glasses, wasn't even at school. Somebody said she was so upset about Kennedy that she stopped eating and got sick and went to the hospital. I think that was a bunch of baloney, but I was glad she wasn't there. I didn't want to run into her again. I stayed away from Mr. Liotta, too.

I got another pair of glasses that week. My father wasn't as mad as I thought he was going to be. I thought he'd kill me when he found out. I told him that I broke them playing football during P.E. when I scored a touchdown. I don't know if he believed me, but at least he didn't get mad.

I bought that Bob Dylan album at Grayson's Music and it was pretty good. Mostly I stared at the picture on the front. My mom heard me playing it and asked what it was and I showed her and she said, "I wouldn't play that when your father's around."

Did she think I was a moron?

Finally, after waiting a whole week, I was going to Greenwich Village to find that place where Jeannie Thomas's brother got a cheap guitar. I almost forgot the name, but then I remembered it was called Max's. When I looked it up in the yellow pages it had the tiniest ad I had ever seen in my life. It was really called Max Valentine's House of Music. I figured I'd buy a guitar and learn how to play it and maybe even enter the talent show. I bet Jeannie and Connie would flip if I did that. One of them might even go out with me, if they broke up with their stupid boyfriends.

I got up real early on Saturday and did all my chores so I could go into the city and get my guitar when the store opened at ten o'clock. Since I was going to Greenwich Village I didn't want to wear my regular clothes. I wanted to look like a folk-singer. I put on these cruddy old blue jeans that my mom saved for when we went camping and an old shirt and this old brown jacket I found in the garage. It looked almost exactly like the one Bob Dylan wore on the cover of that album. I put everything on and looked in the mirror in my bedroom, and I have to admit I looked like a real folksinger. I was headed downstairs, all dressed up, when my father came around the corner. I think he'd been waiting for me.

"Where do you think you're going?"

"Out," I said.

"Not like that you aren't."

"Why not?"

"Because it's not Halloween. You look like a bum! Go upstairs and put on some decent clothes."

"What's the matter with what I'm wearing?"

He crossed his arms. "Nothing. If you're a hobo! Now march yourself back upstairs and change."

I crossed my arms. "They're just clothes."

"Listen, buster, clothes make the man. No son of Harold Johnson is going out looking like a bum!"

My mom came in wearing her robe with her hair up in curlers. "What are you two yelling about?"

My father pointed at me. "Your son has decided he wants to look like Freddie the Freeloader."

Freddie the Freeloader was a character this guy named Red Skelton played on TV. He was a lot more famous than Silly Sammy, the guy with the bananas. Freddie the Freeloader was a bum. He had a beard and smoked a cigar and his clothes were all torn up and dirty. My father loved Red Skelton, but I didn't, because he was always laughing at his own jokes, like he thought he was the funniest guy in the world. Anyway, the point is, I didn't look like Freddie the Freeloader. I looked like a folksinger, but I couldn't tell my father that.

"Is that my old suede jacket?" asked my mom.

I couldn't believe it. I was wearing my *mom's* jacket? I had no idea it was her jacket.

My father looked like he was gonna faint. "You're wearing women's clothes? What the hell is going on here?"

My mom smiled. "Oh, Harold, he's just trying to look like Bob Dylan." Except she didn't say it right, she said "Bob Die-lan."

"It's *Dylan*," I explained. "Not *Die-lan*. And I'm not trying to look like him!"

"Who the hell is Bob Dylan?" asked my father.

I was afraid my mother was gonna say he was the guy we heard on the radio and my father really would've killed me right there.

"He's a singer," I said.

My father shook his head. "This is the dumbest thing I ever heard."

My mother chimed in. "Now don't forget, Harold, you used to dress like Frank Sinatra."

"I did not!"

"Oh, yes, you did."

"I did *not*!"

"Harold, I have photographs."

I couldn't picture my father dressing like Frank Sinatra, in a shiny suit and hat.

My father looked at my mom. "Well, at least Frank dressed in a nice suit! He looked good. He looked sharp." Then he gave me a real disgusted look. "Your son here looks like something out of *The Grapes of Wrath*." *The Grapes of Wrath* was this book that they made us read in eleventh grade. It was really long, but it was pretty good. The people in it were real poor farmers and they wore old ragged clothes. I can bet you my father had never read that book. He never read books. He must have seen that old movie they made out of it. He pointed his finger at me again and said, "I'd rather look like Frank Sinatra than something the cat dragged in!"

And then I said something that I don't know whether I made up or heard somewhere, but it sounded pretty good when I said it. "Don't judge a man by his clothes, but by what he does and says."

My father stared at me for a second and I wasn't sure what he was going to do. It was kind of scary. He finally said, "Well, this man is saying 'Get upstairs and change your clothes if you know what's good for you!'"

I went up the stairs, stamping my feet.

"And don't stamp on the stairs!"

I went into my room and opened my closet. I was just going to put on some regular school clothes and put my folksinger clothes in a bag, but I got a better idea. My father had made such a big deal about my folksinger clothes that I decided to put on the best clothes I had. I put on a white shirt, a tie, my

39

black dress pants, a black jacket, and black shoes. My mother was making breakfast and my father was reading the paper when I came in all dressed up. He looked really surprised. "What are you doing in your church clothes?"

My mom looked up and smiled. "Tommy, you look so nice."

I knew she would say that. She always says that, even when I don't look that nice. Even when I'm wearing stupid stuff and I just have my shirt tucked in.

My father started reading his paper again. "Where're you going?"

I tried to act real casual, like it was no big deal. "Into the city."

"What for, honey?" asked my mom.

"I'm gonna buy a guitar."

My father started laughing this big goofy laugh like when he watches Jackie Gleason in *The Honeymooners* on TV. He loves Jackie Gleason, even more than Red Skelton. I hate *The Honeymooners*. I don't think it's funny at all. Jackie Gleason and his wife live in a really small, really cruddy apartment and all they do, the whole time, is yell at each other. Why would you want to be married to somebody who yelled at you all the time? And Jackie Gleason's got those weird eyes that pop out and he's really fat, but, of course, beautiful women are hanging all over him. He'd just be a big, fat, pop-eyed creep if he wasn't on TV. Anyway, my father finally stopped laughing and said, "What are you gonna buy a guitar for?"

I know I shouldn't have said anything smart-alecky, but I was still kind of mad because I had to change my clothes, so

I said, "Because I want to learn how to play the guitar and I thought it might be easier if I had a guitar."

That was a mistake.

My father slammed the paper down on the table and stood up and his face got all red. "Don't get smart with me, buster, or you'll be sitting on your can, in your room, for the whole weekend!"

We stared at each other for a little bit and then my mom cleared her throat even though I knew she didn't have to. It was pretty fake. "Honey, do you have to go all the way to Manhattan to buy a guitar? Why don't you buy one at Grayson's Music, here in town?"

My father sat down. "Their guitars aren't good enough for you?"

"The guitars are more expensive at Grayson's," I said.

My father started reading his paper again. "I'm not paying for any guitar or any guitar lessons."

"I'm gonna pay for it," I said.

My mom got all smiley again. "Harold, I think this will do Tommy a lot of good. I think everyone should play a musical instrument. I always wished we'd given him piano lessons."

I was *really* glad my parents never made me take piano lessons. You have to play the same stupid notes over and over and play all those boring classical songs and give recitals. And if I was good, they'd probably make me play a duet with that blind girl who always wins the talent shows.

My father pointed at his coffee cup and my mom filled it up. He took a sip and then said, "My parents made me take piano lessons for five years."

I couldn't believe it. He could have said he was an astronaut and I wouldn't have been so surprised. I couldn't even imagine my father sitting at a piano, let alone playing it.

"You played the piano?" I asked.

My mom got all excited. "Harold, you never told me that!"

He put down his cup. "I hated every single second and my parents wasted a lot of money. End of story." He went back to reading his paper.

I headed for the door. "I gotta go."

"Be back by four o'clock on the dot!" said my father.

As I went out, I could hear them both yelling after me.

"Stay away from Forty-second Street!" yelled my mom.

"And Greenwich Village!" yelled my father.

GUITAR LESSON #1

I had tossed the bag with my folksinger clothes out the window, so I picked it up outside and ran down the sidewalk. I got to the bus station and changed my clothes in the restroom. That was kind of creepy. I'd never changed clothes in a public restroom before. I went into one of the stalls and did it as fast as I could. You always hear about creepy guys hanging around in public restrooms and I didn't want to run into one.

I put my church clothes in a locker, but I put my new glasses in my folksinger jacket pocket, just in case I needed them. I didn't want to wear them when I was walking around Greenwich Village. I had to keep wearing the same shoes, but they looked okay since they weren't that nice to begin with.

I got on the bus to go to the Port Authority in Manhattan. I was in my folksinger clothes now and I got some real weird looks from people. One lady even got up and moved away when I sat down next to her. I couldn't believe it. I don't know what she thought I was going to do. That had never happened to me before. It was kind of cool.

I had forty-seven dollars in my wallet. I had been saving up for a long time. I had this stupid idea that I wanted to get a microscope. I had seen some movie where this cool scientist guy had a microscope and I wanted to get one, but then I decided it would get boring pretty quick just looking at stuff. So I just kept saving my money: Christmas money and birthday money and money for mowing lawns and stuff.

I got to the Port Authority and took the subway downtown. I didn't get as many looks on the subway. I came up out of the subway at the West Fourth Street station, which was right in Greenwich Village. I thought I'd see a bunch of folksingers and beatniks, but the first thing I saw was an old guy on a corner handing out pamphlets. He was yelling at everybody, "Join the John Birch Society! Fight the communists! American democracy is crumbling due to the influence of the red left-wingers!"

He probably thought I was a communist because of what I was wearing, so he didn't say anything to me. But he put one of his pamphlets right in my hand and I had to take it because I couldn't drop it and be a litterbug. It was all about how the communists were taking over America. My father would have loved it. I put it in my coat pocket.

It took me about twenty minutes to find Max Valentine's

House of Music. It was a cruddy little store with the name painted on the door. There were a bunch of neat-looking guitars hanging in the window. At the bottom of the window, in the corner, there was this dinky little sign that was all faded so you could hardly read it. There were even some dead flies stuck to the bottom of it. The sign said FREE LESSON WITH EVERY GUITAR SOLD.

I went in and the place was really dark. I felt like I was in a cave. It was kind of scary in a way. There were all sorts of different musical instruments hanging from the ceiling: trumpets and trombones and clarinets and drums. I even had to duck my head a couple of times so I wouldn't bang into them, and I'm pretty short. Way in the back of the store, sitting on a stool, was this little old bald guy I figured must be Max. He was smoking a cigarette and eating a sandwich at the same time. I couldn't believe it. He would take a bite and then take a drag on his cigarette and chew and blow smoke out at the same time. It was pretty disgusting.

He looked up at me and yelled, "Whaddaya want, kid?" He was yelling, like I was clear across the street. I told him I wanted a guitar. He didn't even get off his stool; he just grabbed a guitar that was right behind him, hanging on the wall. "You couldn't buy a better guitar in all of New York City!"

He handed me the guitar and looked at his watch and took a big bite of his sandwich. It was a pretty cruddy-looking guitar. It was probably made in Japan. I looked at all the different parts, pretending like I really knew about guitars, but I had no idea what I was supposed to be looking for. I looked inside the round hole in the middle of the guitar. There was some writing inside and I was trying to read it.

Max was getting impatient. "So? You want it or what?"

I looked at the price tag. It was a little more than I thought it would be, but I had enough money.

"Yeah, I want it." I hadn't even played it. Of course, I didn't know how to play it, but I could have at least strummed the strings or something.

I gave him the money and he put the guitar in this really cheap cardboard case and started to push me toward the door. "I know you two will make beautiful music together!" He was trying to get rid of me like he had to go to the bathroom or something.

"What about my free lesson?" I asked.

"Lesson?" He looked at his watch and let out one of those big sighs. "Oh, yeah. The lesson. All right, sit down."

He pointed at a stool and I sat down and he sat down across from me on another stool. "Now, you must hold a guitar like you are holding a woman."

I didn't know what he meant, but I tried to hold it like I was holding a woman.

He laughed. "You haven't held many women, have you, kid? This isn't a wrestling match! Hold it gently. Now, we'll start with an easy chord. E minor. Beautiful chord. Only takes two fingers to do it right." He winked at me. "Know what I mean?"

I didn't know what the heck he was talking about.

"Put this finger here and that finger there. . . . Press

down. . . . Harder. . . . Now take your other hand and strum it across the strings with your thumb."

It was pretty hard to press down on the strings. It really hurt my fingers. I didn't think it was going to hurt to play the guitar. But when I strummed the strings with my thumb, it sounded really neat. I got all excited and said, "Wow! That sounded great!"

"Don't get too excited, kid! Andrés Segovia isn't out of a job yet!"

Andrés Segovia was this really famous guitar player. He was a Mexican or Spanish or Italian guy and he was supposed to be the best in the world. He was a little bald guy; he kind of looked like Max. I saw him on *The Ed Sullivan Show* once. He played that kind of music that guys stamp their feet to real fast when they dance. I don't like that kind of music, but you can tell you have to be really good to play it.

I played the chord again and the front door opened and in walked a woman. She looked kind of old, but she was trying to look like a sexpot. She had a ton of makeup on and real bright red hair. If you saw her across the street you'd get excited and think she was really sexy, but up close you could see she was pretty old, like thirty-five or maybe even forty.

"Hello, Mr. Valentine," she said in a really fake kind of soft and whispery voice. She sounded like Jackie Kennedy.

Max jumped up off his stool like a rocket. "Hello, Mrs. Davies. You're early."

She started to unbutton her coat. "I couldn't wait."

He gave her a goofy smile. "I know the feeling."

She took off her coat and she had the biggest boobs I had ever seen in my life. They were enormous. Twice as big as Connie Brand's. I couldn't take my eyes off them. Neither could Mr. Valentine.

She lit a cigarette. "You said you had an instrument you wanted to show me?"

Max nodded. "Yeah. In my office."

She blew a ton of smoke out of her nose. She was really good at smoking. "On the desk?"

Max was practically drooling. "Yeah, on the desk."

She started to walk up a little staircase toward a door that had MAX VALENTINE—PRIVATE written on it. Even though she was old, I have to admit she had pretty sexy legs. I mean, she was way too old for me, but to Max, who was even older than she was, it was like Marilyn Monroe was going upstairs.

Max said, "I'll be up in two minutes!"

She gave him a big smile from the top of the stairs and said, "I certainly hope so." Then she went into his office and closed the door. Max just kept staring at the door. I think he forgot I was there. So, I cleared my throat. It sounded even faker than when my mom does it.

He looked at me and yelled, "See ya, kid!" Then he started pushing me out of the store.

"But what about the rest of my lesson?"

"I gotta close!"

"But you only showed me one chord!"

He pushed me out and slammed the door and put up one of those signs that says BACK IN FIVE MINUTES.

LOSING ANN-MARGRET

So, I had a guitar, but I only knew how to play one lousy chord. I figured I could go home and get a book of guitar chords at Grayson's and learn the rest on my own. But I didn't want to go home right away. I figured, here I was in Greenwich Village, I might as well walk around for a while. I had a guitar, I could sort of pass for a folksinger . . . well, almost. My hair was pretty short. I wished I had longer hair like Bob Dylan had on the album cover. I decided I should get a hat. I walked around and found this army surplus store that sold junk from World War II and the Korean War. I went in and they had these cool brown corduroy caps, so I bought one. I bought a pair of sunglasses, too. They were more like Beach

49

Boy surfer sunglasses, but they were pretty tough-looking and I had always wanted to get a pair and they made me look older when I put them on.

When I came out of the store a tour bus was parked outside with all these tourists and a guy talking on a microphone.

"Yes, ladies and gentlemen, here we are in Greenwich Village, the heart of the folk music scene. Famous for its coffeehouses and nightclubs! Keep your eyes peeled for beatniks and folksingers! You just might see Peter, Paul . . . or even Mary!"

I'd seen Peter, Paul, and Mary on *The Ed Sullivan Show* once. Peter and Paul had these weird little beards so they looked like beatniks. Mary was a fox. She had really long blond hair and she flipped it around a lot when she sang. She was wearing a short skirt and she had real sexy legs. My father even noticed. When my mom went out of the room he pointed at the TV and said, "Nice pair of sticks on that broad!"

I didn't think Peter or Paul or Mary would be walking around Greenwich Village, because they were big stars, but you never know, so I looked around a little. The tourists on the bus were looking around like crazy. You could tell they were dying to see a folksinger. One of them even leaned out of the bus window and took a picture of me. I couldn't believe it.

I was kind of getting tired of walking around and I wanted to go home and try to learn a song. Maybe I'd even take my guitar to school on Monday and just walk around with it. I wasn't sure where the closest subway station was, so I asked an old lady who was standing on the sidewalk.

"Excuse me, ma'am? Which way is the subway?"

She looked at me and then she made a face and said, "Damn kid!" Then she spit on the sidewalk. A real big loogie. I had never seen a woman spit before. She almost hit my shoe. It was pretty disgusting. I started to walk away when a negro kid came up to me. He was about my age, maybe a little older, and really big. I was a little scared, even though he had a big smile on his face.

"Looking for the subway? Follow me, man. I'm going to the subway."

I didn't want to follow him. I said, "Uh, well, I'm not going right now."

He could tell I was afraid of him. He nodded his head and kept smiling.

"That's cool. You a folksinger?"

I couldn't believe it. He thought I was a folksinger. I smiled a big goofy smile and then tried to look serious.

"Yeah. I'm a folksinger."

It sounded really stupid when I said it out loud.

"Cool," he said, and then he stood real close and tapped my guitar case. "Could I see your guitar?"

"Uh . . . yeah . . . sure." I opened the case real quick so he could see the guitar and then shut it. I was still a little nervous. The price tag was still on the guitar and it was poking out of the case.

"You just buy it?" he asked.

"Yeah."

"That's a real nice guitar, man."

"Thanks."

"You know how to tune it?"

"Don't they come already tuned?"

He laughed a little and I could tell that it was a really stupid question.

"If you want me to, I can tune it for you," he said, and pointed over to an alley. "Over there."

"In the alley?"

"Yeah, man. It's too noisy out here on the sidewalk. C'mon."

He started walking toward the alley. I followed him even though I didn't want to. I wanted to get on the subway and go home. But I didn't, and if I *had*, none of the really crazy stuff would have happened. We walked about halfway down the alley and it was a lot quieter. He was whistling. I felt really stupid for being afraid of him.

"Are you a folksinger, too?" I asked.

"No. I'm a thief." He pulled out a knife. It was little, but it was big enough to scare the hell out of me. "Gimme your wallet!"

I couldn't move.

"Come on! Hurry up!"

I held out my wallet and he grabbed it and put it in his pocket. My parents had given me the wallet for Christmas two years ago. It was a really nice leather wallet and it had a neat secret compartment. As soon as the guy put it in his pocket I knew I'd never see it again. There was six dollars in it and my library card and my student body card. But the only thing I was thinking about was a picture I had of Ann-Margret, from that movie *Bye Bye Birdie,* that was in the secret compartment. Ann-Margret has red hair, she's stacked, and she has the sexiest legs I've ever seen. That scene in the movie where she took off her clothes underneath her sweater made me go crazy. I saw the movie with my parents and I was getting all excited and I was sitting right next to my mother, which made me really uncomfortable. Anyway, it was so stupid, I was being robbed and all I was thinking about was my stupid picture of Ann-Margret.

"Gimme the guitar," said the negro guy.

I stopped thinking about Ann-Margret.

I couldn't let him have my guitar. It was going to solve all my problems. Even though he had a knife and my heart was going a million miles an hour and I thought he might kill me, I tightened my grip on the handle of the case.

It didn't do any good.

He hit me in the stomach with his left hand and I doubled over and made a face like Lee Harvey Oswald when he got shot. It really hurt. Even worse than when Janie Workman slapped me. I couldn't breathe. It felt like the time I fell out of my cousin's tree house when I was a kid.

The guitar case opened and the guitar went flying out and the guy grabbed it. I kept holding on to the case and he ran away down the alley with my guitar.

I started yelling all those dumb things that people yell in the movies. "Help! Police! Stop that guy! Help!"

I was so mad. I threw the empty guitar case down on the ground as hard as I could. I felt like crying, but I didn't. I looked up and saw the crazy old spitting woman standing at the end of the alley, watching me. I thought she was going to spit at me again, but she didn't. She just shook her head and said, "Damn niggers."

I just wanted to go home, but there was another woman who had seen the guy running away and heard me yelling, and she got a policeman and he asked me all these questions. He was a big, giant cop. He kind of looked like Freddie Blassie, that wrestler who bites people.

"Can you describe the assailant, kid?"

"He was a negro."

"What a surprise. And . . . ?"

"And what?"

The cop let out a big sigh and scratched the back of his head. "Was he tall? Short? Fat? Skinny? Old? Young? You know how many negroes we got in New York City?"

I shook my head. "No, sir."

"Too many! Go on. What'd he look like?"

"My age, I guess. Seventeen or eighteen, maybe. He was taller than me. Kind of big. Short hair, I think."

He pulled out a little pad and started writing stuff down. "What was he wearing?"

"Uh, I think he had on a red jacket . . . or . . . maybe it was purple?"

"You try to fight him?"

"No. He had a knife."

"Smart move. Probably would've killed you. Okay, what's your name and phone number in case we find something?"

I didn't want him calling my parents. My father would probably get mad at me. I just wanted to forget the whole stupid thing. I said the first name I thought of, which was the name of the moron flag monitor.

"Ray Gillette."

"That French?" asked the cop.

"I don't know."

The cop looked at me funny. "You don't know if your last name's French?"

I am so stupid. "Uh, yeah. It is."

I gave him my grandmother's phone number and he put away the pad he was writing on. "Look, he's probably already sold it or pawned it for dope by now. Tough luck, kid. Little advice: stay out of alleys."

He got in his police car and drove away.

The crazy old spitting woman had been watching and she looked at me and said, "Damn cops." Then she spit in the street again and walked away.

I didn't feel so good. I was all hot and sweaty and I felt like maybe I was going to throw up. I hate throwing up. I'll do anything not to throw up. I started to take big breaths and I felt a little bit better. I sat down on some steps in a doorway. I wanted to find that negro kid and kill him. It had taken me so long to earn all that money. And I had wasted it all on a stupid guitar. I was such an idiot to think girls would like me if I was a folksinger. I was still a creep. It didn't matter if I put on different clothes and played a guitar, I would always be a creep. I looked down at my guitar case on the ground. My *empty* guitar case. This was the dumbest thing I had ever done in my whole dumb life. It was even dumber than when I raised the flag back up and told that joke to Janie Workman. I wanted to jump off the George Washington Bridge again.

But then I met Angelina.

A REAL LIVE GREENWICH VILLAGE GIRL

"You got a cigarette?"

That was the first thing she said to me.

I was looking down at my guitar case on the sidewalk, so the first thing I saw was a pair of boots. Then I looked up and saw she was wearing those black things like ballet dancers and trapeze people in the circus wear on their legs. She had great legs. As good as Ann-Margret's. I looked up some more. She was wearing this big baggy sweater that just kind of hung down. She had on a long raincoat that was unbuttoned and she had her hands jammed in the pockets. She had long, straight black hair parted in the middle, and she was wearing sunglasses.

56

"Cigarette?" she asked again.

A real live Greenwich Village girl was talking to me. I couldn't believe it. She reached up and pulled her sunglasses down a little and peeked over the top of them. She was really pretty.

I was trying to think of something cool to say. I wished I was smoking and could give her a cigarette. I wished that I had been like Billy Barkley and had learned how to smoke. I wouldn't have even cared if my grandfather had spanked me in front of a friend.

I couldn't think of anything cool to say, so I said, "Cigarette?"

She smiled. "Yeah. Cigarette? You know? Those little pieces of paper with dried tobacco leaves inside? You light them on fire and suck on them and blow out the smoke?"

I laughed a little bit. "Sorry, I don't sm—"

I couldn't tell her I didn't smoke! It looked like practically everybody in Greenwich Village smoked, and I bet every single folksinger smoked. I started to pretend to look for a pack of cigarettes, going through all my pockets.

"Sorry. I don't have any left. I smoked a whole pack this morning. I usually smoke two or three packs a day. I just smoked my last one."

I looked down and saw a cigarette butt on the ground. I pointed at it. I didn't think she really believed I smoked and I thought that would prove it.

"There it is. Right there."

I can't believe I said that. Then I saw there was red lipstick on the cigarette.

I am such a stupid jerk.

She took off her sunglasses and brushed back her hair. She was so pretty it almost hurt to look at her.

"What's your name?" she asked.

"Tommy."

I couldn't *believe* I said "Tommy." That's what my *mother* calls me. I sounded like I was five years old when I said it. My voice was all high. I tried to make my voice real low and it sounded even dumber.

"Thomas."

Nobody called me Thomas.

"Tom."

She smiled again. She had the greatest smile I had ever seen.

"Well, it's nice to meet you, Tommy Thomas Tom." She ran her hand through her hair. "My name's Angelina."

Angelina. The name fit her perfectly.

"You want a pear?" she asked.

I hate pears.

"Yeah," I said. "I love pears."

She reached in her raincoat pocket and handed me a pear. "You live in the Village?"

"Sure. Yeah. Of course." I couldn't believe I was saying this.

"Yeah. Me too. It's a cool place to live. I go to N.Y.U."

"Cool."

"So, you're a folksinger?"

SHE THOUGHT I WAS A FOLKSINGER!

"Yeah."

"Have you gone to see Woody?"

I had no idea who she was talking about.

"Woody?" I asked.

"Yeah," she said.

"Woodpecker?"

She laughed. "No. Woody *Guthrie*."

Since she had laughed, I pretended that I had been making a joke all along. "I was kidding."

She nodded. "I was thinking about going to see him up in that hospital he's in."

Now, I didn't even know who Woody Guthrie was. And I didn't want to go see some guy I didn't know in a hospital. I hate going to hospitals. It's so depressing. My parents made me go to see my grandfather in a hospital once. It smelled bad and you could see bags of pee hanging on the sides of beds and it made me want to barf. I really hoped Angelina wasn't going to ask me to go see this guy with her. I knew I'd barf if I saw one of those bags of pee. That would be terrific, barfing in front of a beautiful girl and some guy I didn't know.

Later on I found out that Woody Guthrie was this famous old guy who started all the folksinging stuff and wrote about a million songs. He was really sick with some bad disease in a hospital in New Jersey and people would go visit him. Even Bob Dylan went to see him in the hospital and he'd sing Guthrie's old songs to him. Now I wish I would have visited him.

Anyway, I said, "I haven't seen Woody yet. But I'm going to. I plan to. Soon. Real soon."

She sat down next to me. *Really* close. I couldn't believe it.

Her shoulder was almost touching my shoulder. "So, what kind of songs do you sing, Tom?"

"Uh . . . folk songs."

She laughed. She looked pretty when she laughed. "You're funny. Seriously, what kind of songs do you sing?"

I didn't know what to say. I mean, what other kind of songs were there? I thought maybe it was a trick question or something, so I just said, "Good ones."

"What clubs do you play at?"

"The good ones."

She nodded. "What kind of guitar you got?"

"Uh, just a regular old guitar."

She touched the guitar case with her hand. She had the most beautiful hands I'd ever seen. I never really paid much attention to girls' hands before. Even that girl's hand I tried to hold at that boring football game wasn't that special. I can't remember if it was a pretty hand or just a normal hand. But Angelina had unbelievable hands. You could tell by just looking at them that they were always soft and they never got sweaty or clammy. My hands were clammy all the time. I was always wiping them on my pants.

Angelina was kind of tapping on the guitar case with her fingers. I started to get worried because I thought she was going to open it up.

"So, Tom, what kind of guitar is it? Martin? Gibson?"

"Yeah. A Martin Gibson."

She laughed again.

I should've told her the guitar had just been stolen. Maybe

she would've felt sorry for me. But I didn't want to take the chance. I had to change the subject.

"So, Angelina, what do you do?"

"I'm a poet."

"Cool," I said.

"And an actress."

"Cool," I said again.

"And a dancer and a painter."

"That's cool."

I couldn't stop saying "cool."

"But mostly I'm a poet."

"Poetry's cool."

I had never said the word "cool" so many times in my entire life.

"You want to hear one of my poems?" she asked.

"That'd be cool."

I *had* to stop saying "cool."

She reached into her purse and pulled out this big notebook. She opened up the notebook and pulled out a piece of paper.

"It's called 'Land of the Free?' There's a question mark after 'Free,' so it's a question, not a statement."

I nodded my head. I was afraid if I opened my mouth I'd say "cool" for the ten millionth time.

She started to read her poem:

America is the land of the free,
That's what my teachers always taught me

To be an American is to be lucky
Because all Americans are free
But it doesn't look that way to me,
Take a look around and what do you see?

"That's a great poem," I said.
　"I'm not done."
　"Sorry."
　She was kind of bugged I had interrupted her, but I really
thought it was over. Most of the poems I knew were pretty
short.
　She went on.

That's an American sitting in the back of the bus
That's an American going to a different school than us
That's an American sitting way up in the balcony
That's an American has to use a different door than you and me
That's an American drinking from a different water fountain
That's an American whose vote nobody's countin'
That's an American who can't move in
To some neighborhood 'cause of the color of his skin
That's an American being beaten by a cop
Knocked down by a fire hose so he can't get up
That's an American hanging from that tree
That's an American who's supposed to be free
But it doesn't look that way to me
You say America is the land of the free
It doesn't look that way to me.

I wasn't sure if she was done, so I didn't say anything. I really wanted to be sure she was finished. Finally she closed her notebook and looked up at me.

"Angelina, that was great."

"Really? You think so?"

"Yeah. I really dug it."

"I know it rhymes, which is really old fashioned, but I'm trying to get away from that. My next poem isn't going to rhyme."

"How many have you written?" I asked. I hoped she had a million more, because I could have sat there forever, with her right there next to me, just listening to her read poems.

"I've written about fifty or sixty."

"Let me hear 'em."

She laughed. "Right now?"

"Yeah!"

"You're putting me on. I can't read them all here." She flipped through her notebook. "I'm writing a new one about President Kennedy getting killed. It's not done yet. Man, I still can't believe that happened."

I nodded my head. "Yeah. I can't believe it happened, either."

Another one of those tour buses came by with tourists taking pictures out the windows. Angelina gave them a real dirty look and stuck her tongue out. "I *hate* those damn buses. All those stupid tourists with their cameras, coming down and taking pictures of us like we're in the zoo or something. It's such a drag."

"Yeah, man, it's a real drag," I said. I was trying as hard as I could to sound like a folksinger. I wasn't really sure how folksingers talked, but I figured they were sort of beatnik types and they all said "drag" and "man" a lot.

All of a sudden she put her hand on my knee.

No girl had *ever* done that to me.

I thought I was gonna die right there.

"So, Tom, where's your pad?"

And then I did the dumbest thing. I started to look through my pockets. I thought she wanted a pad of paper to write something down. Maybe she had thought of a new poem about the tour bus or something. Of course, she meant a *pad* like an *apartment*. I tried to pretend I was looking for cigarettes again. "Sorry, I thought I had one more cigarette. Uh, my pad is a couple blocks away."

She stood up. "Cool. Why don't we go hang out there? I'll read you some more of my poems and you can sing me some of your songs and then . . . whatever?"

I couldn't believe she said that.

I said, "Okay."

I couldn't believe *I* said that. I felt like I was in some weird dream. I stood up and she grabbed my arm with both of her hands and kind of squeezed it a little. We started walking down the sidewalk.

Together.

This beautiful girl was walking with me, holding on to my arm and smiling, and the wind was blowing her hair and it was *just like the album cover!*

I could have walked with her for the rest of my life and been completely happy. Until I remembered:

I didn't have an apartment in Greenwich Village.

I didn't know how to play the guitar.

All I had was an empty guitar case.

I had to think really fast.

WHERE WAS GODZILLA?

"Uh, Angelina, I just moved into my pad and it's a real mess. I haven't unpacked yet and I don't have any chairs. Why don't we go to *your* pad?"

I thought this was a brilliant idea. We could go to her pad, she would read me some more poems, I could tell her about losing the guitar so I wouldn't have to sing any songs, and then . . . whatever.

"We can't go to my pad, Tom. I live in a dorm at N.Y.U. No boys allowed. It's a drag. We could sneak in, but my roommate's sick."

We were walking through Washington Square Park where they have that big round fountain. We walked by these three folksingers. *Real* folksingers. One guy was playing the guitar and a girl was playing the banjo and another guy was singing. They nodded at me when I walked by and I nodded back. I guess folksingers did that when they saw each other.

Angelina said, "Hey, man, I don't mind a mess. We can sit on the floor. Let's just go to your pad."

I had to think of something. Really quick. I stopped walking and hit my forehead with the palm of my hand like they do in the movies. It felt so fake.

"I completely forgot. They're fumigating my pad today. I've got cockroaches. I mean, my pad's got roaches. We can't go there."

She looked really disappointed. "That's a drag. Well, hey, why don't you sing me a song right here?"

She tapped my guitar case again.

My *empty* guitar case.

"You want me to sing out here?"

"Yeah."

I couldn't go on like this. I had to tell her the truth. Well, I had to tell her *part* of the truth.

"Angelina, I have a confession to make."

"What?"

She was looking up at me and standing pretty close. She smelled *really* good. I let out a big sigh and said, "Somebody stole my guitar this morning."

I opened the guitar case and showed her. She looked really sad. I thought she was going to start crying or something.

"Oh, no! What a drag. I *really* wanted to hear your songs."

I nodded my head. "I *really* wanted to play them for you."

Right then I was so glad my guitar had been stolen. We just stood there for a while and I pretended to be upset.

Then all of a sudden she said, "Wait a minute!" She let go of my arm and ran over to the group of real folksingers that I had nodded to. I couldn't hear what she was saying to them, but the one guy handed Angelina his guitar and they all started walking toward me.

I couldn't move.

My feet felt stuck to the sidewalk and all I wanted to do was run away as fast as I could.

"This guy says you can use his guitar," said Angelina as she handed me the guitar and took my empty guitar case.

"Thanks," I said.

I started to look at the guitar the same way I did when I was at Max's music store, pretending I knew what I was doing. I turned it over and looked at the back. I could kind of see my reflection in the shiny wood. There was my stupid hat and my stupid surfer sunglasses and my stupid face.

Why was I doing this?

Why was I pretending to be a folksinger?

Why was I here in Greenwich Village?

Why wasn't I at home sitting on the sofa watching TV like every other Saturday?

I knew I couldn't just look at the guitar forever. I had to do something. But I couldn't think of anything to do. I was hoping something crazy would happen, like all of a sudden there would be a riot, or the Russians would bomb us, or Martians would land, or Godzilla would attack.

No such luck.

I had to say something. "Cool guitar."

"Thanks, man," said the guy whose guitar it was.

Some other people started to walk over to see what was going on. A little crowd was forming around me.

"Play something," said the banjo-playing girl.

I just kept looking at the guitar.

Where were the Russians?

Where were the Martians?

Where was Godzilla?

"C'mon, man, give us a song," said the guitar-playing guy.

"Where'd you get it?" I asked.

"Max's."

I got all excited. "Really? You know Max? He's great! I bought my first guitar from Max! He gave me my first lesson!"

"Let's hear a song!" somebody shouted.

I was sweating like when I mow the lawn. For the first time in my life I wished that I was mowing the lawn, and I *hate* to mow the lawn more than anything.

"How old is your guitar?" I asked.

"Hey, man, are you gonna play or not?" asked the guy whose guitar it was. He was getting all mad. I thought folk-singers were supposed to be nice.

Somebody said, "What's the matter? Don't you know how to play?"

I looked at Angelina. I could tell she was kind of wondering what was going on. It was the worst moment of my life. I had to do something. I was about to give the guitar back and just run away. Then somebody yelled at me from across the street and saved my life.

"Hey, kid!"

This little guy was running across the street toward me. He looked about thirty, and he wore a suit and a tie and he was smoking a cigar. He grabbed my arm and said, "My boss needs a picture of a folksinger and you're the lucky guy!"

He dragged me across the street to another guy who was standing next to a big giant camera on one of those three-legged stands.

"What do you think?" asked the grabby guy.

"Horrible. He's perfect," said the camera guy. "Okay, let's go, it's getting late. You, Mr. Folksinger, stand over there next to the model and look depressed."

I hadn't seen the model at first, but there she was, standing on the sidewalk. She was wearing a really fancy black dress, the kind rich women wear to the opera or a funeral or something. She was really tall and had on a ton of makeup, especially around her eyes. She was really pretty, of course. She kind of looked like Ann-Margret, except she didn't have red hair.

Angelina and the folksingers were all acting cool, like it was no big deal, but they all crossed the street to get a better look.

The model was staring at me. "Did I see you at Folk Town last Saturday?"

I shook my head. "No, I don't think so."

"Maybe it was at the Factory with Andy?"

I didn't know what she was talking about, but I didn't care. I was standing next to a real live model who looked like Ann-Margret and nobody was yelling at me to play a song. She turned to the camera guy and said, "Hey, I got an idea!"

The camera guy crossed his arms and glared at her. "Really? You got an idea? I got an idea, too, honey. Let's shoot this so we can get the hell out of here! I'm freezing my ass off!"

The model started whining. "C'mon, it's a fabulous idea!"

The camera guy sighed. "The model's got a fabulous idea."

"Let's have him sing a song while we shoot!"

Why did she have to say that?

She was all excited and said, "He can play a song while I move around him! I'll act out his anger, his angst, and his rebellion! It'll be fabulous!"

She grabbed my arm. "Sing something."

I felt like I was going to throw up again.

Angelina and the real folksingers and some of the other people who were watching started to clap.

"Hold it!" yelled the camera guy. He pointed his finger at me. "Kid, I want a picture, not a concert. If you play any of that commie folk crap, I'll kill ya."

I was *really* glad he hated folk music.

The folkie guitar guy went up to the camera guy and said, "What's the matter with folk music?"

"Everything!" said the camera guy. "Beginning with the fact that it ain't music!"

"It's the greatest music there is!" yelled the banjo girl. "What kind of music do *you* listen to?"

"None of your business!"

"I bet he listens to that old fogey Frank Sinatra!" said the guitar guy.

The camera guy got real mad. "You say anything about Sinatra and I'm gonna punch you all the way to Cuba!"

The guitar guy got right in the camera guy's face and said, "Frank Sinatra is a no-talent, prehistoric, washed-up, bourgeois pig!"

The camera guy's face was getting really red. "You little punk, I oughta knock your block off!"

"Go ahead and try it, pops!" yelled the guitar guy.

And then the camera guy slugged the guitar guy right in the face. The guitar guy was really surprised. You could tell he didn't think the camera guy was going to hit him. It looked like it really hurt. A lot more than when Janie Workman slapped me at school.

The banjo girl took off her banjo and tried to hit the camera guy with it. Then the grabby guy grabbed hold of her banjo and she started to kick him to get it back. The model started screaming and crying. I put down the guy's guitar, grabbed Angelina's hand, and we beat it out of there fast.

BIGTOWN

We just started walking and I didn't know where we were going, but I didn't care. At least nobody was asking me to play the guitar. Angelina stopped for a second and pointed at this bar called the White Horse Tavern.

"You ever go here?"

"Uh, not as much as I used to."

"Didja know that's where Dylan Thomas drank himself to death?"

I nodded. "Yeah. I heard that."

"I love Dylan Thomas."

"Me too."

I had no idea who Dylan Thomas was. I looked in through

the door of the White Horse Tavern. It was pretty dark inside and kinda depressing. And the fact that some guy drank himself to death in there made it even more depressing. I don't know why people go into bars and just sit there and drink. I tried to drink a beer once with Billy Barkley when I was fourteen. It was the worst thing I had ever tasted. He finished his, but I couldn't finish mine. Last year, when my mom wasn't around, my father gave me a sip of the drink he always drinks when he comes home from work, which is Scotch on the rocks. It was even worse than the beer. Billy Barkley said you have to learn how to drink stuff like that. He said he was going to do it when he got older.

We started walking again and Angelina said, "Dylan Thomas is my favorite poet. Dickinson is great, too, and the Beat poets, Ginsberg and Ferlinghetti. Who's your favorite poet?"

Believe it or not, I actually did have a poet I thought was pretty good. His name was Carl Sandburg. He wrote that poem that they make you read in school about fog being like cat feet. That poem was okay, but some of his other stuff was really good. I didn't say he was my favorite poet, though, because I didn't know whether she would think he was cool enough. I finally just said, "You know, there are so many great poets it's hard to pick one."

We walked a little more and then all of a sudden she said, "Feel my hands," and put both her hands on my face. One hand on each cheek. They were ice cold, but I didn't care. "You wanna get some coffee, Tom?"

I hated coffee. I don't know how people drink that stuff.

"Sure," I said. "Coffee sounds great. We can get some coffee. Where do you wanna go?"

"Have you ever been there?" she asked, pointing at this place across the street. It was called the Nouveau Folk Café. It had a sign with a painting of a naked girl with really long hair, like Lady Godiva, playing a guitar and it said LIVE FOLK MUSIC. It was a pretty cruddy sign. It looked like somebody had just painted it and they weren't a very good artist.

I shrugged. "Sure. This looks okay."

I went inside my first coffeehouse. It was pretty dark, but not as bad as the White Horse Tavern. I took off my sunglasses so I could see. There were all these really weird paintings on the walls that looked like little kids had painted them or like somebody had just thrown some paint on a piece of cardboard and then put it in a frame. There was a dinky little stage at one end of the room. They had a real moose head up on the wall, with one of those Mexican hats on it and a really beat-up guitar hanging around its neck. There were only four people in the whole place. A waiter, two guys playing chess, and a really crazy-looking bald guy who was reading a book about ten thousand pages long. Angelina and I sat at this little table that had an empty wine bottle on it with a candle stuck inside.

This waiter, who seemed pretty mad for some reason, came up to our table. "Whaddaya want?"

"Double espresso," said Angelina.

I didn't know what to order. They had these little menus on the table, but they were written in Italian, so I didn't know what anything was.

"I'll just have some water, please," I said.

The waiter tapped the menu with his pencil. "Minimum charge is fifty cents per person, Mr. Getty."

He was trying to be a smart-ass by calling me Mr. Getty. J. Paul Getty was the richest guy in the world. I read that he had a pay phone in his house for people to use because he didn't want to pay for long-distance calls. If I was the richest guy in the world, I wouldn't do that. How cheap can you be?

"I'll have an espresso, too," I said.

"Double?"

"Sure."

The waiter went away. I had no idea what I had just ordered, but I guess I was gonna get two of them. I looked back at Angelina and she was kind of staring at me.

"You know something," she said, "you remind me of somebody."

I hoped she was gonna say Bob Dylan, but I had a bad feeling she was gonna say somebody else. She kind of squinted and said, "That guy on TV with the bananas."

I knew it. No matter how hard I tried, no matter what I did, probably even when I was sixty years old, I was *always* gonna look like Silly Sammy.

"You mean Silly Sammy?" I asked.

"Yeah. He's really cute," she said. "I used to have the biggest crush on him."

I couldn't believe she said that!

She put her elbows on the table and cupped her face in her hands. She could be on the cover of a magazine.

"So, where are you from, Tom?"

I couldn't say New Jersey. I was trying to think of a place that folksingers came from. On the back of the Bob Dylan album it said he was from Minnesota, but I didn't want to be from the exact same state so I said, "Nebraska."

"What city?" she asked.

I couldn't think of a single city in Nebraska. I should have at least known the state capital because they made us memorize all of them when I was in fifth grade. I finally just made up a name and it was the dumbest name I could have possibly thought of.

"Bigtown."

"Bigtown?"

"Yeah. Bigtown, Nebraska."

Every time I heard it, it sounded worse.

She smiled a little and said, "I've never heard of it."

Of course she hadn't! It was the world's stupidest name for a city that I had just made up!

"Uh, not many people have heard of it. It's not very big."

I couldn't believe I said that.

Angelina looked really confused. "So why do they call it Bigtown?"

"Well, uh, it's a little place, but the pioneers that started it called it Bigtown because, uh, they thought it was going to get big, but it never did." I *had* to get her to stop asking questions. "Where are you from?"

She leaned back in her seat. "New York."

"Cool," I said. I figured it had been a long time since I had said "cool," so it was okay to say it again.

The waiter brought the double espressos. It was a real gyp.

They were in these dinky little cups and they didn't even fill them up to the top. Angelina put sugar and milk in hers and started stirring it with this little spoon. "Have you been in any marches?"

Marches? Why was she asking me about marches?

I said, "I was going to be in a Fourth of July parade with the Boy Scouts, but I quit before they had the parade."

"No, I meant civil rights marches."

She must have thought I was the stupidest folksinger she had ever met.

"Have you been down south and marched?" she asked.

"Uh, I haven't marched yet, but I've been meaning to."

I would *never* go down south to be in a civil rights march. I've seen them on TV and they've got police dogs attacking people and the police turn fire hoses on people and knock them down and hit people with nightsticks. Marches are really dangerous, you could get killed. I think negroes should have civil rights and everything, but I didn't want to get killed over it. Angelina said she wanted to go down south. I nodded like I did, too.

I took a sip of the espresso. It was the worst thing I had ever tasted in my life. It was horrible. I couldn't believe that people paid to drink it.

Angelina brushed back her hair with her hand. I thought it was really sexy when girls did that. Of course, the girl had to be pretty to look sexy when she did that, and luckily Angelina was.

She took a sip of her espresso and said, "I was at the March on Washington in August. It was so incredible. Martin Luther

King Jr. spoke and Dylan sang. There were over two hundred thousand people there. When my father found out I was there, he had a cow. He almost killed me. My parents are something else. My mother's all right, I guess. But my dad is your typical right-wing, Republican, John Birch Society, conservative reactionary." She leaned across the table and whispered, "I don't tell many people this, but I think he works for the C.I.A."

I got really excited. The C.I.A.! That was like James Bond. If my father worked for the C.I.A., that would be the coolest thing ever, I'd be telling everybody I knew.

"Is he a spy?" I asked. "Does he carry a gun? Has he ever killed anybody?"

She shrugged. "I don't know. Probably. It's not something I'm proud of. He's such a hypocrite and a phony."

I was glad she didn't know she was sitting directly across from a phony folksinger. She looked at her watch and stood up. I thought she was going to leave because I hadn't ever been in a march, but she just said, "I gotta make a phone call and get some cigarettes. I'll be right back."

Dang it! Now I was going to have to smoke a cigarette, too.

I watched Angelina walk away and I couldn't believe how great she looked. What I really couldn't believe was that she was here with me. I guess I could pretend to smoke a cigarette so I could be with her a little longer.

The angry waiter guy came up. "You want anything else, Rockefeller?"

"No, thanks," I said.

He tore the bill off his little pad and tossed it on the table.

It almost went in my cup of espresso, which was practically full, but I caught it before it did. I reached for my wallet in my back pocket.

It wasn't there.

I usually keep my wallet in my back pocket, but my father says that if you're in the city you should always carry it in your front pocket so nobody can pickpocket you.

I reached into my front pocket.

Nothing.

JINGLE BELLS

I had completely forgotten that that negro guy had stolen my wallet. I started to get mad again because I remembered that the jerk had my guitar, my money, my library card, my student body card, and my picture of Ann-Margret.

The mean waiter guy crossed his arms and tilted his head to the side. "Problem?"

"Could I have a glass of water, please?" I asked.

He shook his head and walked away.

Okay. Now I was dead. All I had was two dimes and Angelina was gonna come back any minute. I thought about just running out of the place. I had never done that before, but I knew people who would eat and then just run out of a place without paying. They called it dine and dash.

I looked around to see where the mean waiter guy was so I could figure out when I should get up and run. I was looking at the front door and wondering how fast I could get there when the door opened and all these people came barging in. It was like a hundred Japanese tourists. They all had cameras and looked really excited. There was a tour guide, one of those big smiley guys, and he was talking really loud.

"Here we are, ladies and gentlemen, an authentic Greenwich Village coffeehouse! Espresso, cappuccino, and other exotic drinks available! The live entertainment begins momentarily. We're running a little late, so you have ten minutes and then you must be back on the bus or you'll have to stay here and become beatniks!"

The tour guide started laughing like this was the funniest joke in the world. All the Japanese tourists stared at him for a second and then they must've thought it was the funniest joke in the world, too, because they all started laughing. The tour guide guy grabbed the mean-looking waiter, who it turned out was the owner of the place, and dragged him over near where I was sitting and started yelling at him.

"Frank, where the hell is the creep who's supposed to be singing up there?"

"The S.O.B. moved back to his parents' apartment on Park Avenue."

"Listen, Frank, you told me if I brought my buses in here to buy your funny coffee, there'd be some of that authentic folk crap!"

The tour guide started poking his finger into Frank's chest really hard. It looked like it hurt. One time my P.E. coach, Mr. Vujovich, did that to me when I forgot my jockstrap.

"Johnson! Where's your jockstrap? You can't play unless you got a jockstrap! Did you forget to tell your mommy to give you your jockstrap? Don't tell me you forgot it or you will be giving me four laps!"

He was jabbing me in the chest the whole time he was yelling at me. The next day I had a big bruise on my chest where he poked me. It hurt for like a week.

Anyway, the tour guide was poking Frank, the waiter-owner guy, really hard now. "Listen, Frank, in fifteen minutes I gotta get these Japs up to Forty-seventh and Broadway to see a matinee of *Oliver!*"

"He ain't here! What am I supposed to do?"

The Japanese tourists were starting to clap and chant, "Folk song! Folk song!" The tour guide's face was turning red. I thought he was going to have a heart attack. "You get a folk-singer on that stage or starting tomorrow I take all my tour buses somewhere else!"

"Gimme a break! I ain't got a singer!"

Then the tour guide pointed at me, sitting there with my guitar case. "What about him?"

Frank looked at me all smiley. "Hey, kid, how'd you like to get up and sing a couple of songs?"

I couldn't believe this was happening.

"No, thank you," I said.

Frank stopped smiling. "What? Kids pay *me* to sing here! You can sing for free! Just get up there!"

"I really don't want to."

He grabbed the bill and tore it up. "Your drinks are on me. C'mon, all I need is one lousy song. *Capiche?*"

"I . . . I don't know that song," I said.

The tour guide leaned over the table. I thought he was going to start poking me in the chest. "One song, kid."

Frank grabbed my arm and started dragging me toward the stage.

"Sir, I *really* can't do it. I don't have a guitar." I opened my guitar case and showed him it was empty.

Frank dragged me over to the moose head and grabbed the guitar that was hanging around its neck. He threw it at me and I barely caught it.

The tour guide guy slapped Frank on the back. "Good work, Frankie! I'm going next door for a real friggin' drink. See you in ten minutes!"

Frank dragged me up on the little stage. He was really strong for a little guy. The tourists all started clapping and taking pictures.

I had to tell him the truth. "Mister, I can't do this."

"You know how many kids would give their right arm to sing here?"

"I'm not one of those kids. I don't know how to play the guitar and I can't sing."

He leaned real close and whispered in my ear. "Kid, if you don't sing, I'm gonna break your arm."

Then he turned to the audience and got all smiley again. "Ladies and gentlemen, the Nouveau Folk Café is proud to present one of the finest folksingers in all of Greenwich Village."

The Japanese tourists got all quiet and just stared at me.

"He's here in New York City all the way from . . ."

He looked at me and I said, "New Jersey."

He made a face and said, "He's from Texas!"

The Japanese tourists all said, "Ah! Texas!"

"And his name is . . ." He turned and looked at me again.

"Tom," I said.

"Will you please welcome Ramblin' Tom Frost!"

The Japanese tourists shouted out, "Ramblin' Tom Frost!" Then they all leaned forward in their seats. I looked over at Frank, who was standing at the side of the stage waiting to break my arm.

"I don't know what to sing!"

"Kid, I don't care what the hell you sing! You can sing 'Jingle Bells' for all I care! Just sing!"

I looked down at the guitar. It only had four strings on it. I knew that a guitar was supposed to have six strings, but since I didn't know how to play the guitar, it didn't matter if it had four or four hundred. The only thing that mattered was that I had to sing and pretend to play the guitar or that Frank guy would break my arm.

And where was Angelina?

How long did it take to buy a pack of cigarettes and make a phone call?

I tried to remember where that Max guy had told me to put my fingers for E minor. Did you put one finger on the first fat string or the second one? I think it was the second one. Did the next finger go on the string next to the other string? And was it one of those little squares down from the top of the guitar or two? I finally just guessed. I put my fingers on the strings and hoped that it was E minor.

I closed my eyes and started to strum. It sounded horrible. It was the worst-sounding thing you have ever heard, but I just kept strumming.

I looked over at Frank and I could tell from the way he was looking at me that he realized that I'd been telling the truth and I couldn't play the guitar.

Then I forgot how "Jingle Bells" started. I had sung "Jingle Bells" about a million times in a million Christmas programs when I was a kid and I couldn't remember the first words. After what seemed like about an hour I finally just started in the middle.

> *Jingle bells, jingle bells*
> *Jingle all the way*
> *Oh what fun it is to ride*
> *In a one horse open sleigh*

"Hey!" shouted all the Japanese tourists.

They knew the song.

I remembered the beginning:

> *Dashing through the snow*
> *In a one horse open sleigh*
> *O'er the fields we go*
> *Laughing all the way*

"Ha! Ha! Ha!" shouted the Japanese tourists again.

They all started clapping along. I kept playing. I couldn't believe it. It was the worst music you have ever heard in your life. The crazy-looking bald guy got up and left. The chess players gave me these really dirty looks. I was hoping that I would finish the song before Angelina came back. I didn't want her to see me singing "Jingle Bells" and playing that guitar with four strings. I started to sing and play faster and Frank gave me a real dirty look. Then all of a sudden the front door banged open and the tour guide came running in, yelling. "Okay! Okay! Show's over! Time to move! Go see *Oliver!* Broadway! Let's go!" He started pulling the tourists out of their seats and pushing them toward the door.

Frank ran up to him. "What the hell are you doing? They haven't even ordered their drinks!"

"If these Japs don't see *Oliver!* it's Pearl Harbor all over again! I got a schedule to keep. Let's go, people! Chop-chop! Time to see *Oliver!* Pretty songs! Pretty costumes!"

I stopped playing and all the Japanese tourists applauded and cheered and started shouting, "Tom Frost! Tom Frost!"

I guess I was a folksinger.

CONFESSIONS

I got off the stage as fast as I could and saw Angelina trying to come back in the front door while the tour guide was pushing all the tourists out. I put the guitar down on a table, grabbed my empty guitar case, and pushed my way through the tourists to Angelina.

"Did you just play?" she asked.

"Yeah. Sort of."

The Japanese tourists were all still cheering and clapping as they walked out of the coffeehouse to their bus. As we walked outside behind them, I saw this guy with the biggest beard I had ever seen wearing one of those little French hats and talking to the tour guide.

"What happened?" asked Angelina.

"The guy asked me to sing and he had a guitar so I sang a song."

"What'd you sing?"

I decided to tell her the truth. " 'Jingle Bells.' "

She laughed. She looked so great when she laughed. "You're pretty funny. What'd you really sing?"

" 'Jingle Bells.' "

"Are you kidding me?"

"No. I sang 'Jingle Bells.' They loved it."

She nodded. "Right . . . that's perfect. Those tourists wouldn't get it if you sang one of your real songs. It'd go right over their heads. 'Jingle Bells.' That's cool." She started to dig in her purse. "I had to go two blocks to find a pay phone and get cigarettes. You want one?"

She held out a pack of Winston cigarettes. That was the kind my aunt Evy smoked. I couldn't pretend to smoke a cigarette. I knew I'd start coughing. All of a sudden I just wanted to tell Angelina everything. It was driving me crazy making up all this stuff and I knew I couldn't keep doing it. I had to tell her the truth.

"Listen, Angelina, I gotta tell you something."

She looked up at me with those beautiful eyes. "Tell away."

I was about to tell her I was the world's biggest fake. I was going to lose my one and only chance with a girl like this, but I had to do it.

I took a deep breath and said, "I'm not . . ."

"Tom Frost?"

I turned around and saw it was the guy with the big beard and the French hat.

"Can I talk to you for a minute?" he asked.

"Yes, sir?"

He laughed. "A folksinger with manners? You see something new everyday! You new around here, kid?"

"Uh, kinda."

"My name's Manny Adleman. I run Folk Town over on MacDougal. Those tourists really dug you. Why don't you drop in and play a song tonight? We start around midnight." He nodded toward Angelina. "Bring your chick."

I opened my mouth but nothing came out.

"We'll be there," she said.

"Cool. I'll see you then." He walked off.

Angelina grabbed me. "Oh my God! Folk Town! That's the best club in the Village! Tom! You get to play at Folk Town!"

"No, wait. Angelina, I gotta tell you something . . ."

She grabbed my arm. "We gotta celebrate! We'll go back to your place. I bet those cockroaches are dead by now."

We started walking. It was all too good to be true.

She thought I was a folksinger and I was going to sing at the best club in Greenwich Village and she wanted to go to my apartment.

But it wasn't true, and I had to tell her.

"Let's sit down for a second," I said.

"Sit down? How can you sit down at a time like this?"

We were back at Washington Square and I made her sit down on a bench.

"Angelina, I gotta tell you something and you're not gonna like it very much."

"What?"

"Look, you're really great and . . ."

"You got a girlfriend?"

"No. I *wish* I did. I . . . I mean, no, I don't."

"So what's the big deal?"

I took a deep breath.

I looked at her face.

I didn't say anything right away, because I wanted to remember her like this, and I knew that as soon as I told her the truth, it would be all over and I'd never see her again.

"I'm not a folksinger."

She looked at me with this weird expression. "You're not a folksinger?"

"Nope."

"So . . . what are you?"

I told her everything. I told her about the flag and Janie Workman slapping me and the vice principal yelling at me and Jeannie and Connie looking at the Bob Dylan album and dressing up in old clothes and getting the guitar and Max and learning E minor and the woman who spit and getting my guitar stolen and the policeman and the fact that I was a big fake.

"I even wear glasses," I said as I pulled my glasses out of my pocket and put them on. I couldn't look at her. I didn't know what she was going to do. I thought she might hit me or start crying or cuss me out or just run away.

I couldn't believe what she did.

She started laughing.

And she didn't stop. She just kept laughing and laughing. She was cracking up. It was starting to bug me.

"It's not that funny," I said.

"Yes, it is!" she said. She was laughing so hard she was crying. "It's hysterical!"

"No, it's not." I knew it wasn't really funny at all. It was pathetic. This creepy guy trying to look like Mr. Cool and be a folksinger.

She was still kind of laughing, but not quite as hard. She wiped her eyes and caught her breath and said, "It's funny, Tom, it's really funny."

I was kind of getting mad because she was laughing at me. "Tell me why it's so funny."

She reached in her coat pocket and pulled out a pair of glasses and put them on. She still looked pretty. Then she put her hand out.

"Hello, Tom, my name is Penny Clark. I live on Eighty-sixth Street with my parents, I go to Holy Redeemer High School, I'm a junior, and it's very nice to meet you."

GUITAR LESSON #2

I couldn't believe it.

"You're not . . . ? Your name's Penny?"

"Ugh! Don't say it! I *hate* my name! It sounds like a dumb Mouseketeer or some moron cheerleader!"

I didn't remember a Mouseketeer named Penny. I used to watch *The Mickey Mouse Club* all the time when I was a little kid. All the guys liked Annette, but I thought Darlene was the prettiest. Anyway, I didn't think Penny was such a bad name.

"I came down here to meet a folksinger and have an adventure," she said.

That made me feel worse. "And you met me. Sorry."

She laughed again. "Hey, you thought you'd met an N.Y.U. Greenwich Village chick and you met *me*."

I didn't care at all that she wasn't a Greenwich Village girl and didn't go to N.Y.U. She was a girl, she was pretty, and I think she still liked me.

She said, "So, I guess we can't go to your pad and celebrate."

I shook my head. "Nope—wait a minute. Celebrate what?"

"That you're going to play at Folk Town tonight."

I laughed. "Oh, right."

I thought she was joking, but she wasn't.

"You gotta do it, Tom."

"What? Are you crazy? I can't sing at Folk Town!"

"Why not?"

"I'm not a folksinger!"

"You fooled that photographer, you fooled those tourists, you fooled that guy with the beard, and you fooled me!"

"Angelina, I mean, Penny, they just thought I *looked* like a folksinger. I'm a fake. I don't even have a guitar!"

"That's okay. I've got my brother's old one at home."

"But I *can't play* the guitar! I can barely play one chord. I—"

She put her hand over my mouth and said, "Shut up." Her hand was really soft and smelled good and it was warm because she'd had it in her coat pocket. "You know one chord, right?"

I sighed. Just like my mother. "Yeah. One stupid chord."

She stood up. "That's it! All you need to know is how to play one chord!"

"What?"

"I saw Dylan at Carnegie Hall in October and he played a new song called 'Ballad of Hollis Brown.' He only plays one chord the entire song. He never changes. It's the same chord the whole song!"

She ran into the street and started waving her arm around and yelled, "Taxi!" You could tell she was really good at hailing taxis. "Tom, c'mon! Let's go!"

I stood up and said, "Where are we going? I gotta be home by four."

I can't *believe* I said that. It made me sound ten years old.

A taxi pulled over and Penny told the driver, "Eighty-sixth and Park Avenue." She opened the back door of the taxi and got in.

I stood on the curb. "What are you doing?"

"You're gonna sing at Folk Town tonight."

"You're crazy. This is ridiculous."

She looked at me real serious. "You can do it. We'll practice at my house. Nobody's there. My parents are gone for the whole weekend."

I got in the taxi as fast as I could.

I had no intention of singing at Folk Town. That was a real folk club with real folksingers. But I wasn't going to turn down the chance to go to an apartment with a girl whose parents weren't going to be there. I'm not a complete moron.

The taxi was going about ninety miles an hour. I thought we were gonna crash about a hundred times. I was holding on to the strap above the door. Penny was just sitting there like it was no big deal. She probably rode in taxis all the time. I had only ridden in a taxi in New York a couple of times. The few times we did go into the city my father always made us walk or take the subway. Even though I thought we were going to crash, it was cool to be riding in a taxi with a girl. She had her window down a little bit and the wind was blowing her hair. She looked really pretty. In fact, there hadn't been one time, all day, when she hadn't looked pretty.

"So, you can sing, right?" she asked.

"A little bit. But I'm not a great singer."

"It doesn't matter. Neither is Bob Dylan, but he's real."

"But I don't know about singing in front of a bunch of people."

"You sang 'Jingle Bells' in front of a bunch of people, right?"

"Anybody can sing 'Jingle Bells.' You want me to go to Folk Town and sing 'Jingle Bells'?"

"No. I've got a different song." She leaned forward in the seat. "It's right here, driver."

The taxi pulled over and we got out. She paid for the taxi and I looked up at the building. It was a mansion. I couldn't believe we were going in there.

"You live here?" I asked.

"Yeah."

"Are you rich?"

"No. My parents are."

It was the biggest, fanciest, richest house I'd ever been in. I felt like I was in a movie. I kept expecting Cary Grant or James Bond to come out of one of the rooms wearing a tuxedo and drinking a martini. We went in the living room, which was practically the size of my whole house. There were real paintings on the walls that looked like they should be in a museum and big fancy sofas and chairs that I was afraid to sit on.

Penny kicked off her shoes and threw her jacket on the sofa. "We'll work in here. If you leave around three you should be home by four. Then tonight you can sneak out around eleven o'clock and meet me at Folk Town."

I had never snuck out of my house at night in my entire life. Where would I have snuck out *to*? What would I have snuck out *for*?

"Penny, I'm not sure I can do this."

"C'mon, it'll be something you can tell your grandchildren." Then she made her voice sound like a real old person's. "I sang at Folk Town in Greenwich Village, sonny!"

I laughed and then she said, "I'll be right back. Sit down."

She went out of the room and I sat down on the sofa. It was really comfortable. It was so big you could sleep on it if you wanted to. I was hoping Penny would sit on the sofa next to me. Then I could make my move. I wasn't sure what my move was gonna be, but I figured I'd hold her hand first and then put my arm around her and then kiss her.

Maybe.

If I chickened out and didn't do that, I was at least going to ask her to the Tom Turkey Dance. The school had postponed the dance when President Kennedy was shot and they were going to have it in two weeks.

She came back in with her brother's guitar. She took it out

of its case and it looked brand new, like nobody had ever played it. She put it down on the sofa and started going through this really old desk that looked like Ben Franklin had used it. "I think my father has an old harmonica in here somewhere. He used to play it when I was a little kid."

"I had a harmonica when I was a kid," I said.

I didn't tell her it was just a stupid little toy harmonica that I got for Christmas in my stocking. It was plastic and green and had a picture of a cowboy on it. I couldn't play any songs, I just blew into it, the same note over and over. My dad finally threw it away because I played it all the time and it drove him crazy.

Penny got all excited. "You played harmonica? That's great!"

I knew I shouldn't have told her about the harmonica.

"I wasn't very good. I couldn't play it very well."

"You don't need to. You just blow into it every once in a while."

On top of the Ben Franklin desk were pictures of Penny's family. They were the kind of pictures you see in magazines when they do stories about famous people. She told me who they all were. There was one of Penny when she was a little girl standing with her brother, who was a lot older than her. He looked like a nice guy. He was making this goofy kind of face and he had his hand on top of Penny's head and you could tell she thought that he was pretty funny. There was a picture of her parents at some big fancy dinner, all dressed up. Her mother was really pretty, the Miss America type, but older. Her father kind of looked like my P.E. coach, Mr. Vujovich, the guy who was always poking people in the chest. He had a crew cut and was real tan and looked about seven feet tall. You wouldn't want him mad at you.

Penny found her father's old harmonica. I wasn't too crazy about playing it because you had to put it in your mouth and who knows what kind of germs he might have.

"He hasn't played this in a hundred years," said Penny.

That made me feel better.

"I'll make a harmonica holder out of a coat hanger so you can play it while you're playing the guitar."

"I have to play them at the *same time?*"

"Don't worry. I'll show you."

She reached into her brother's guitar case and held up a little piece of plastic. "Here."

"What's that?"

"A pick."

"What's a pick?"

"You use it to play the guitar. Watch." She strummed the strings on the guitar with the pick. I tried it and the pick fell out of my fingers into the hole in the middle of the guitar. I tried shaking the guitar upside down, but I couldn't get it out.

"Maybe I should just use my fingers?"

She shook her head. "No. You have to use a pick."

She got the pick out of the guitar and then she sat down right next to me, really close, and held the pick in my hand to show me how to do it. I still couldn't believe how soft her hands were and how good she smelled. I could have sat on that big sofa learning how to hold a pick for the rest of my life.

"Good," she said. "Now you have to start working on the song."

"What song?" I asked.

" 'Land of the Free.' "

I started to get nervous again. "I've never heard of it. You want me to sing a song I've never even heard?"

"Calm down. You did hear it. Well, you heard the words at least. It's the poem I read to you."

She held out a piece of notebook paper that said "Land of the Free by Penny Clark" and on the top, in red ink, was a big F.

"You wrote this for school?" I asked.

"Yeah."

"And you got an F on it?"

"That's because my English teacher, Miss Fat Head No Brain Idiot Harding, said it was 'un-grammatical *and* un-American'! It was the best poem and she wouldn't even let me read it to the class!"

"You want me to sing a poem that you got an F on?" As soon as I said that I knew I shouldn't have said it. "Sorry. I didn't mean it like that. I meant I don't know how the song goes."

"Don't worry, you can just 'talk' it. You don't really even have to sing. Half the folk songs are just talking anyway."

"Okay."

"Practice your chord."

I started to put my fingers on the guitar and I stopped.

"What's the matter?" she asked.

"I forgot where to put my fingers."

I tried a couple of different ways and then I finally remembered the right place. "Penny, I'm gonna forget. I know I'm gonna forget."

She kind of rolled her eyes and said, "Don't move your fingers."

She went out of the room. I honestly thought about leaving. This whole idea was crazy. But I was alone in an apartment with a really pretty girl. How could I leave?

She came back with a bottle of red fingernail polish. She started painting two red dots on the guitar, right under the strings, where I was supposed to put my fingers. I couldn't believe she was putting fingernail polish right on the guitar.

"Do you think that's a good idea?" I asked.

"Yeah. Just put your fingers right where the dots are."

"No, I mean do you think you should be doing that to your brother's guitar? If it was my guitar I wouldn't want someone putting fingernail polish on it." I was really worried about her brother's guitar. I didn't even know the guy, but I felt bad she was doing this to his guitar.

"Don't worry about it," she said.

"But that'll never come off. Won't your brother mind?"

"No."

"*I* would."

"He won't."

"How do you know?"

"I just do."

"But this is a *really* nice guitar! I bet he's gonna be mad."

"No, he won't."

"Yes, he will."

She closed up the little bottle of fingernail polish and stared at me for a second and then she said, "He's not gonna be mad because he's dead and dead people don't get mad."

At first I thought she was making a joke and I started to laugh, but then I could tell by the way she was looking at me that she wasn't. I felt like the biggest, stupidest, most idiotic, jerkiest creep of all time. I didn't know what to say. People always say stuff like "I'm sorry," but that didn't sound right to me. Finally I said, "How'd he die?"

"In the Korean War."

"Oh."

I saw a movie about the Korean War called *Pork Chop Hill* when I was about thirteen with my father. When it was over I said, "I wanna join the army when I get older." My father looked at me with this really serious expression and said, "No, you don't." Then he bought me a banana split on the way home, and he never did stuff like that.

Anyway, Penny looked like she didn't want to talk about her brother, so I decided not to say anything else. She handed me the guitar and said, "Here. Blow on the nail polish so it dries."

I blew on the red dots and she started copying her poem down, in real small letters, on one of those little three-by-five cards. She changed some of the words so it would sound more like a folk song than a poem. Then she Scotch-taped it to the top curvy part of the guitar so I could look down and read it.

"You can probably memorize it by tonight, but if you forget any of the words, you can read off this."

She got a coat hanger and twisted it around so it held the harmonica and then she bent it some more so it could go around my neck. I couldn't believe she could do all this stuff.

"When do I blow on the harmonica?" I asked.

"Do it in between the verses, whenever you're not singing."

"Okay."

I knew I wouldn't be able to do any of this stuff she wanted me to do in a million years. It was impossible. But I started strumming down on the strings and I have to admit it didn't sound too bad. Penny sort of half sang and half talked the words. It actually kind of sounded like a real song. It wasn't great, but it wasn't horrible. It was a lot better than anything Jeannie Thomas or Connie Brand could have come up with for the talent show.

Penny sang it about three times and then I kind of sang it with her and then she said, "Okay, now try it alone."

She jumped up off the sofa and grabbed my hand and pulled me over to the middle of the room. "Ladies and gentlemen, Folk Town is proud to present Tom Frost!"

I started to strum the guitar and the stupid pick fell in the hole again.

She was going to tape the pick to my fingers, but I said I wouldn't drop it anymore. I tried singing the first lines of the song. It didn't sound too bad. At least it didn't make you want to throw up or anything. After the second verse Penny said, "Blow on the harmonica."

I stopped strumming and blew on the harmonica.

"Don't forget to keep playing the guitar."

"Penny, I can't do both at the same time."

"Just try it."

I did. It sounded horrible.

She said, "We'll work on that."

Then I sang, or really I talked, the rest of the song. I couldn't believe I got all the way through it; most of the time I had to look down and read the words on the card she had taped to the guitar. When I finished and looked up at Penny she was nodding her head and smiling.

"We did it! You're a folksinger!"

She ran over and hugged me. The guitar kind of got in the way, but I didn't care. I knew this was the moment to make my move and I had to act fast. It would have been kind of hard to try to kiss her with the guitar in between us, so I decided to ask her to the Tom Turkey Dance first. If she didn't want to go to the dance with me, I knew there'd be no way she'd want to kiss me.

"Uh, Penny? There's this dance at my school that's coming up, and I know you probably think things like that are stupid, it's got a pretty stupid name, the Tom Turkey Dance."

"You're right. That's a pretty stupid name."

"Yeah. I know. But would you, maybe, want to go with me? I mean, we wouldn't have to stay very long, you could leave whenever you wanted to."

"Sure."

"Really?"

"Yeah."

"Yeah?"

"I'm not lying."

Then she didn't say anything. She just looked at me and I
just kept looking at her.

I had to kiss her.

I could tell she wanted me to.

I was finally going to kiss a girl.

A pretty girl.

A *really* pretty girl.

And then her parents came home.

I HATE FOLKSINGERS

We heard them arguing outside as they walked up to the front door.

"Are you going to pout for the rest of your life, Miriam?"

"Maybe I will, Oscar, maybe I will!"

Penny and I both sort of froze. We heard the key turning in the lock and she said, "Oh my God! What are they doing here?" I thought I should hide somewhere, like under the sofa, and I asked Penny if I should, but she just stared at me and said, "What are they doing here?" again.

The front door opened and we heard them in the front hallway.

"I don't know why you're so upset," said her father.

"Oh, really? You don't? Maybe it's because we just walked out of someone's house after being there for only fifteen minutes!"

"I'm not spending the weekend with people like that!"

"They were just playing some music!"

"Music? It was that same folk crap that Penny plays all the time!"

I *knew* I should have hidden under the sofa.

Penny hadn't been making stuff up when she had told me about her father being a right-wing, conservative guy. And he was just about to see a folksinger, or at least a guy pretending to be a folksinger, in his living room with his daughter.

They started walking down the hallway toward the living room.

"They were nice people and you were rude to them," said Penny's mother.

"Nice people? They're probably having Fidel Castro over for a barbecue next weekend!"

I didn't know much about Castro except that he was a communist and he had some missiles in Cuba and everybody was afraid he was gonna shoot them at us, but President Kennedy made him get rid of them. Cuba was also where they had the Bay of Pigs, which, of course, was also the punch line of that joke my father told and then I told to Janie Workman and that started all this.

Anyway, Penny's parents came in the living room and they both looked pretty much like they did in the picture I had seen on the desk, except a little bit older. Her father wasn't seven feet tall, but I bet he was at least six feet four. There I was in all my folksinger stuff, holding a guitar, with a bent coat hanger around my neck with *his* harmonica in it and my stupid hat on. When he saw me his face got all weird and he said, "What the hell is going on here?"

Penny moved away from me and said, "Daddy, I thought you were staying—"

Her father grabbed me and shoved me against the wall. "Who is this creep?"

"Daddy, don't!" said Penny.

"Oscar, let go of that boy!" said her mother.

He was squeezing my arms really hard. Then I remembered that Penny said she thought he was in the C.I.A. and I got really scared. He could probably kill me with his bare hands.

"Did you touch my daughter?"

"No, sir," I said.

"Don't give me that 'sir' crap, you beatnik!"

"Daddy, you're so out of it," said Penny. "He's not a beatnik, he's a folksinger!"

Did she *want* him to kill me?

He looked at me like he was going to bite my head off and said, "I hate folksingers."

I had to say or do something fast or this guy *was* going to kill me. My hands were in my coat pocket and I felt this piece of paper. It was the pamphlet that the guy who was yelling about communists had given me when I first got off the subway that morning. I got an idea.

I looked her father straight in the eye and said, "I couldn't agree with you more, sir. I hate folksingers, too."

Both he and Penny said, "What?" at the same time.

I took a deep breath and then just started talking as fast as I could, trying to remember what that guy who had given me the pamphlet had said.

"My name is Tom Johnson and I'm doing a report for my school on the crumbling of American democracy due to the influence of communists and left-wingers in folk music. I was down in Greenwich Village, working undercover, infiltrating their nests." I opened my guitar case and showed him it was empty. "See, I don't even have a guitar. It's all a fake." Penny's father looked a little less mad, but I kept talking. "You have to know the enemy to fight it, sir. I was just telling your daughter that I hope for a career in the C.I.A."

Penny looked at me like I was insane.

Her father didn't look so mad anymore, but I still kept talking. "I'd love to stay and chat, sir, but I have a John Birch Society meeting that I'm going to be late for. May I leave this pamphlet with you?" I pulled the flyer out of my pocket and held it out to him.

He looked down at it and then he said, "Uh, sure. Gosh, son, I'm sorry, I—"

I held up my hand and gave him a big smile. "No need to apologize, sir. If I had a daughter as lovely as yours and I saw her with someone who looked like me, I would have done exactly the same."

Her father smiled and put his arm around my shoulder. "Now this is the type of young man I like to see you with, Penny!"

I shook hands with her father and gave him a real firm handshake. "Nice to meet you, sir." Then I gave her mother a big smile. "Ma'am." Finally I turned to Penny and said, "Nice to meet you, too, Miss Clark."

She gave me a funny smile and said, "I hope to see you again at a later date."

Then she shook my hand and I felt her pass me a little piece of paper. I took it and put it in my pocket. Then I grabbed my guitar case and turned like they do in the army and kind of marched out of the living room, down the hall, and out the front door as fast as I could.

I was walking pretty fast in case Penny's father figured out I had just made all that stuff up and ran after me with a gun. I'm sure he had one in his house. I was really glad to get out of there. I couldn't believe he had fallen for what I said about doing a school report about communists and folksingers. I have to admit I faked it pretty well, considering I'm not an actor.

The piece of paper that Penny slipped to me when we shook hands was her poem with the big red F on it. I figured that she gave it to me because she wanted me to keep working on the song at home. When she said, "I hope to see you again at a later date," I knew she meant that night at Folk Town. I started to think about actually going there and singing the song just so I could see her again. I was trying to figure how I could sneak out of my house without my parents knowing when all of a sudden this big church bell clock started ringing. I looked up and saw it was three-fifteen. I had to be home in forty-five minutes or my father would kill me. I had to go all the way back down to the Port Authority to get the bus to

New Jersey. Luckily I still had twenty cents in my pocket for the subway and my return bus ticket. I took the subway down to Forty-second Street, but I didn't know how to get to where the buses were and I got kind of lost, so I had to go up to the street. As I was coming out of the subway entrance, this police car pulled over right next to where I was on the sidewalk. For a second I thought that Penny's father had found out I was making all that communist stuff up and had called a cop and I was going to get arrested.

"Hey, kid!" shouted the policeman in the car. It was the same one who I had talked to when my guitar got stolen. "I thought it was you! This must be your lucky day."

He got out of the car, and I couldn't believe it, he had my guitar!

He pointed to the backseat of his police car, where a really scared-looking negro kid about my age was sitting.

"This kid said he bought it from some guy for five bucks," said the cop.

"I did!" said the kid in the backseat.

The cop shook his head. "How many times have I heard that cock-and-bull story?" Then he leaned down to the back-seat car window. "You all want your civil rights, don't you? Well, you don't have the right to steal a guitar, punk."

"I didn't steal it!" said the kid.

"Did he have my wallet, too?" I asked the cop.

The cop shook his head. "Nope. They usually spend the money and toss it."

"I didn't steal his wallet or his guitar!" said the kid.

I looked at the kid's face. He wasn't the guy who had stolen my guitar. That guy was older and bigger. "Excuse me, Officer," I said, "that's not the guy."

"I told you I didn't do it!" shouted the kid.

"Shut up!" said the cop. Then he turned to me and smiled. "Take another look, son. I don't think you got a good look at him."

I looked at the kid again and shook my head. "That's not him."

"You sure?"

"Yes, sir. I'm sure."

The kid started yelling. He was mad. "See? I told you I didn't do it! You have no right to arrest me like that. You cops are all the same. Now let me outta here before I call the NAACP!"

The cop looked down at the sidewalk for a while, like he was staring at something, and then he looked back at the kid in the backseat. "So why'd you try to grab my gun when I arrested you?"

The kid in the backseat looked really scared now. "What? I . . . I didn't grab for your gun." Then he looked at me and said, "I didn't go for his gun! I swear!"

I was pretty sure he hadn't tried to take the cop's gun. Why would he do something stupid like that? It didn't make any sense. The cop was twice as big as he was. I felt bad for the kid, but I didn't know what to do. I had already told the cop that he wasn't the guy who had stolen my guitar. He was gonna arrest him no matter what I said.

The cop looked at me and smiled. "Take your guitar and go home, kid." Then he got in his car, started it up, and they drove away. The kid in the backseat looked like he was crying, but I couldn't be sure.

I put my guitar in the case and went into the station. Riding back home on the bus I wondered what was going to happen to that kid. I figured he'd be okay since they couldn't prove he grabbed the cop's gun unless they had his fingerprints on it. His lawyer would probably think of that. They'd have to give him a lawyer, even if he couldn't afford one. You always see that on TV. The lawyer would tell him they had to have his fingerprints on the gun and then he wouldn't have to go to jail.

I really wanted to tell Penny what had happened. Halfway across the bridge heading back to New Jersey, I decided for sure that I was going to sneak out and meet her at midnight and sing that song so I could see her again. I kept reading her poem over and over, trying to memorize it. I hoped she was still going to meet me tonight. And I hoped that kid got a good lawyer.

ROUND MIDNIGHT

When I came home my father was sitting in his chair, like he always does, in the living room reading the newspaper. My mom was sitting in her chair sewing a button on a shirt and humming to herself.

My father looked at me over the top of his paper. "So, let me see this guitar you wasted your money on."

I took it out and showed them.

"Oh, honey, it's beautiful," said my mom. I knew she'd say that, even if it was the crummiest-looking guitar in the world. "Play something for us, Tommy."

"He just got the damn thing," said my father. "How's he supposed to play it?"

"I'll play it after I've practiced," I said.

I went upstairs to my room and practiced playing my E-minor chord. It was harder to press the strings down on my guitar than on Penny's brother's guitar. I just kept singing the song over and over. It started to sound like a real folk song, and for the first time I thought I might be able to pull it off.

Maybe.

To be honest, I didn't care that much about the song. I just wanted to see Penny again. But it was weird because the more I played the guitar and practiced the song, the more I wanted to sound good.

My parents usually went to bed at ten o'clock. I knew they'd be asleep by eleven, so all I really had to do was wait. After dinner I watched a little TV with them so they wouldn't think I was up to anything and also because my fingers were sore from playing the guitar. They watched the same shows every Saturday night. Of course my father had to watch *The Jackie Gleason Show* with bug-eyed Jackie Gleason, yelling and screaming, and all those beautiful women around him. Then my mom liked to watch *The Defenders*, which was this boring lawyer show. Then they watched *Have Gun, Will Travel*, a western that was pretty good, actually, and that ended at ten. Toward the end of *Have Gun, Will Travel* I did a couple of fake yawns. "I'm pretty tired. I think I'll go to bed."

"Good," said my father. "Tomorrow, after church, you and I are going to pull out all the hydrangea bushes in the backyard."

I hated doing yard work. Especially with my father. He mainly just yelled at me whenever we did stuff in the yard. He'd tell me to do something and I'd start to do it and I wouldn't do it right or he wouldn't like the way I was doing it and then he'd yell at me and end up doing it himself and I'd just stand there and watch him. But I wasn't thinking about doing yard work. I was thinking about seeing Penny that night and singing that song. If I pulled this off, it would be the greatest thing I had ever done in my life.

I got in bed and pretended to be asleep. My mom poked her head in my room and came in and kissed me on the forehead. She did that every night. I don't think my father knew. If he did, he would have told her to stop treating me like a baby. I didn't mind it that much. When she left my room, as soon as I heard her walk down the hallway and close her door, I jumped out of bed. I had all my folksinger clothes on again and I was ready to go. I opened my door and peeked down the hallway and waited till my parents' bedroom light went out. I waited about five minutes to make sure they were asleep and then, for the very first time in my life, I snuck out of my house. It was weird walking down the street, with my guitar case, late at night. It was really quiet and dark. All the lights in the houses were out and it seemed like the whole town was asleep.

It was kind of creepy taking the bus and the subway late at night, but it felt kinda cool, too. Some of the people were weird-looking. I just sat there and kept reading Penny's poem over and over so I wouldn't forget any of the words. I probably looked pretty weird, too. When I got off in Greenwich Village, even though it was practically midnight there were people all over the place, walking around and eating in little cafés and going into clubs and stuff.

All of a sudden I realized I didn't know where Folk Town was. It was getting close to midnight and I started to get worried that Penny was already there and she might think I had stood her up and leave. I was gonna find a phone booth and look up the address in the yellow pages when I saw this person walking toward me and I figured I could just ask them where Folk Town was.

At first I thought it was a girl, because the person had really long hair. It came all the way down to their shoulders and it was all black and stringy. But when I saw the face I could tell it was a guy. I'd never seen a weirder-looking guy in my whole life. He had the biggest nose I'd ever seen. A hundred times bigger than mine. It honestly looked like a bird's beak. He made *me* look like a movie star. He was dressed in this old brown suit and had on a blue shirt and a pink tie with a picture of a woman hula dancing on it. He was carrying a brown shopping bag. He was the weirdest person I had ever seen in my whole life and I really didn't want to talk to him, but I figured he probably knew where Folk Town was.

"Excuse me?" I asked. "Do you know where Folk Town is?"

"Why, yes, of course I do!" he said. He sounded really excited when he talked and his voice was really high. For a second I thought that maybe he was a woman, just a really, really, really ugly one. "Folk Town is right around the corner. Are you a performer?"

"No . . . I mean, yeah, I guess I am."

"I am too! I'm a singer!"

Then he reached in his shopping bag and pulled out this old sweater, like the kind my grandfather, the one who died, used to wear, and inside the sweater was a ukulele, one of those little guitars they play in Hawaii. He started to play the ukulele, and I have to admit he was pretty good. But then he started to sing, and he sounded exactly like a girl. I had to get out of there.

"Uh, sorry, I have to go. I gotta meet somebody," I said. "Thanks."

He didn't get mad. He just stopped singing and said, "You're very welcome! Good luck and God bless!"

When I finally got to Folk Town there was a big line of people waiting to go inside. All of a sudden I wanted to throw up. Why were all these people here? I started to think that maybe somebody famous was going to be performing. That made me even more nervous than I already was. I looked around for Penny and couldn't find her. I started to think that she had changed her mind or maybe her father had caught her sneaking out. If she didn't show up, there was no way I was going to do this.

As I was standing around waiting, I kept seeing people looking at me. That was weird. People never look at me. Maybe it was because I had a guitar case and they were trying to figure out if I was somebody famous. They'd look at me and I'd look at them, and when they saw that I wasn't famous, they'd look away, kind of like they were disappointed. I did see other people with guitar cases, *real* folksingers, going inside Folk Town.

A big black car that kind of looked like a limousine pulled up in front. I thought somebody famous might get out, but it was just a bunch of businessmen in suits. I couldn't see all of them, but I didn't see anybody famous.

It was getting pretty late and I was almost thinking about going home when a taxi pulled up and Penny got out, carrying her brother's guitar in a case. She gave me a hug and I didn't think about going home anymore.

She was all excited. "Sorry I'm late! My idiotic parents finally went to bed fifteen minutes ago. They *never* stay up this late. Hey, you found your guitar!"

I told her all about the negro kid in the backseat of the police car and how he wasn't the guy who stole my guitar and how the policeman took him away and she got really mad. She said that tomorrow we'd have to go find out where they took the kid and find the policeman and tell the cops that it wasn't the kid who stole my guitar.

I didn't know how we could do that, and there was no way I could come back to the city the next day, but I said, "Okay."

"That's why you *have* to do my song, Tom! That's what it's all about."

I started to get nervous again.

She said, "I brought the harmonica." She held up the coat hanger with the harmonica on it and put it around my neck. I had really hoped she wouldn't bring it. It was going to be hard enough to do the song without having to worry about playing the harmonica, too.

"Did you practice the song?" she asked.

"Yeah."

We decided I'd use her brother's guitar since it had the fingernail polish dots on it and the three-by-five card with the words taped on it and because it was a million times better than my cruddy guitar.

"You okay?" she asked. "You look kinda pale."

"I'm fine," I lied.

"C'mon, let's go inside."

"Penny, if they find out I'm not really a folksinger, they can't arrest me, can they?"

She started laughing. "You crack me up."

We went inside.

TOM FROST: LIVE!

The place was crammed with people. Every single chair was filled and people were standing along the wall. It was really smoky. It seemed like every single person in there was smoking. The stage was a lot bigger than the one at the Nouveau Folk Café and the whole place was a lot nicer. There was a guy onstage playing the guitar and singing. He was really good. He was playing the guitar really fast and singing really loud.

Manny, the guy with the big beard who had asked me to play, came up to us as soon as we walked in.

"Where the hell have you been?" he asked.

I started to answer but he said, "Follow me." He led us back to this door next to the stage.

"You're on after the next act," said Manny. Then he turned to Penny and said, "Sorry, honey. Only performers back here."

Penny gave me another hug. "Good luck. You're gonna be great."

I went inside this dinky little room in the back where the other performers, the *real* performers, were waiting to go on. There were two other guys with guitars, looking real serious. There was a skinny guy with a banjo who was wearing glasses and smoking a pipe. In the corner was a girl with really long hair that went all the way down past her waist. She was holding an Autoharp like my sixth-grade teacher, Miss Pippin, used to play. When Miss Pippin played the Autoharp she would sit on the front edge of her desk and cross her legs. I sat in the front row so I had a really good view. She had really sexy legs, almost as sexy as Ann-Margret's. But the weird thing was, Miss Pippin wasn't good-looking at all. Her eyes were kind of crossed and she had zits and her hair was weird and she was as flat as a pancake, but her legs were so sexy that you forgot about all the other stuff. I always wondered if she thought that since she wasn't good-looking but had great legs she should show them off as much as possible. She sure sat on her desk a lot.

Anyway, I opened the guitar case and pulled Penny's brother's guitar out. I made sure the little card with the words on it was taped on real well so it wouldn't fall off. The guy with the banjo gave me a dirty look. You could tell he didn't think it was cool to have your words on a card. I didn't care. I was real glad to have the words there in case I forgot something.

I was getting really nervous. I felt like I was gonna have a heart attack. I started walking back and forth, which was kind of hard because the room was so small. I heard Manny introducing the next act and I looked through this little curtain to see who it was. It was the weirdest thing I had ever seen. First I thought it was a girl, because of what he was wearing and how he looked, and then I realized it was a guy. He was wearing really tight black pants and a black-and-white striped shirt. He had clown makeup on his face, but he wasn't acting like a clown. He wasn't saying anything. He was just moving around the stage and pretending to do stuff.

"What's wrong with him?" I whispered to the girl with the Autoharp, who was watching, too.

She looked at me real snotty and said, "Nothing's wrong with him. He's a mime."

"What's a mime?" I asked.

"One who acts without words."

"Why . . . ?"

She looked at me like I was the dumbest person in the world. "It's a universal language, understood throughout the world. Mime is the art form of the future. Someday mimes will be everywhere."

I sincerely doubted that, but I didn't say anything to her because she looked ready to clobber me with her Autoharp. I do have to admit the mime guy was pretty good at what he was doing. It really looked like he was getting trapped inside an invisible box.

Finally the mime guy finished his act and bowed and people clapped and he walked off the stage and went right past me. He was all sweaty and had really bad B.O.

Manny jumped up on the stage. "Okay, next up we've got a newcomer to Folk Town. Will you please welcome Mr. Tom Frost!"

I heard people clap, but I just stood there. I couldn't move.

"Are you Tom Frost?" asked the Autoharp girl.

I nodded.

"Then get out there."

She pushed me toward the stage. You had to walk up a step to get on the stage and she pushed me so hard I almost tripped. By the time I got there people had stopped clapping and it was really quiet. The lights were so bright it hurt my eyes. I couldn't see anybody in the audience, which was good, except I kind of wanted to see where Penny was. I looked down at the guitar and made sure my fingers were on the red dots. I started strumming the strings. It sounded okay, but kind of quiet. I kept staring down at the guitar and strumming. I heard some guy in the audience whisper, "Doesn't he know any other chords?"

I wanted to say, "No, I don't! I just got this guitar today! I have no idea what I'm doing!"

But I didn't.

The tips of my fingers started to really hurt because I was pressing so hard, but there was no way I was going to move my fingers off of those strings. It was getting really hot up there. It felt like they had turned the heater on full blast. I could feel my face getting all sweaty. I decided I better start singing. I raised my head up and saw that I was about a million miles away from where the microphone was. I kept strumming and moved over to the microphone. Somebody in the audience

124

clapped and somebody else laughed and I heard someone say, "Shut up!" I think it was Penny.

I took a deep breath and started to sing:

> America is the land of the free,
> That's what my teachers always taught me
> To be an American is to be lucky
> Because all Americans are free
> But it don't look that way to me,
> Take a look around and what do you see?

My throat felt really dry. I swallowed a couple of times. I looked down at the words taped to the guitar and started singing again.

> That's an American sitting in the back of the bus
> That's an American going to a different school
>   than us
> That's an American sitting way up in the balcony
> That's an American has to use a different door
>   than you and me
> That's an American drinking from a different
>   water fountain
> That's an American whose vote nobody's countin'
> That's an American who can't move in
> To some neighborhood 'cause of the color of his
>   skin
> That's an American being beaten by a cop

Knocked down by a fire hose so he can't get up
That's an American hanging from a tree
That's an American who's supposed to be free
Take a look around and what do you see?
Lot of Americans and they ain't free
You say America's the land of the free?
It don't look that way to me
No, it don't look that way to me.

Finally, after what seemed like about a hundred years, I finished the song.

I stopped strumming and took my fingers off the dots.

Dead silence.

Nobody clapped or booed or threw stuff or anything.

I turned around and ran off the stage as fast as I could.

And then I heard the noise.

People started clapping and whistling and yelling. The banjo player with glasses nodded his head as I passed by and said, "Great song, man!"

The Autoharp girl was all smiley and said, "That really got me."

The mime guy even patted me on the back. I was all hot and sweaty and I just wanted to get outside. I went out of the little backstage room and I saw a door and pushed it open. It led to the alley behind the club where all the trash cans were. It was nice and cool out there. I leaned against a wall and tried to catch my breath. I kept saying to myself, "I did it. . . . I did it. . . . I did it."

The door opened and out came Penny, who was even more excited than I was. She hugged me *again*. I think she had hugged me six times so far that day. I was kinda embarrassed when she hugged me because I was all sweaty, but she didn't seem to mind.

"Tom! You were so great!" she said in my ear.

"I was so nervous."

"You were wonderful!"

"I felt like I was gonna throw up!"

She laughed. "I'm really glad you didn't."

"Me too."

"You *did* forget to play the harmonica."

I couldn't believe it. I had completely forgotten about the harmonica. It was still hanging around my neck.

Penny smiled. "It doesn't matter. Hey? My song wasn't too bad, either."

I was such a moron. I hadn't said anything about her song! "Penny, your song was great! That's why they were clapping so much."

She hugged me *again*. "So, where do we go to celebrate?"

"Celebrate?"

"Yeah, let's go somewhere, get some coffee."

I didn't want any coffee, but I did want to stay with Penny. I knew I couldn't. "I gotta go home. If my parents find out I'm gone, they'll kill me!"

I gave her back her brother's guitar and the harmonica and took my guitar from her.

"Oh, c'mon, Tom, just for a little bit!"

"Penny, I can't. Really."

She sighed. "Okay. But first I want to give the famous new folksinger Tom Frost a kiss from his biggest fan."

I COULDN'T BELIEVE SHE SAID THAT.

I definitely had time for a kiss.

"Okay," I said, trying to be cool. "If you insist."

"I do."

She closed her eyes. I didn't close mine. I wasn't going to miss this.

"Mr. Frost?" said a deep voice.

JOEY MARTINO'S CHIMPANZEE

I looked over and saw a big guy in a shiny suit that must've cost a hundred bucks. "My name is Bob Precht and my boss wants to meet you."

"Uh . . . I'm sorry, sir, I have to go home."

He crossed his arms, just like the cop. "I think it would be a good idea for you to meet him."

"I really gotta go."

He put his arm around my shoulder. "My boss gets upset when I don't do what he tells me to do."

"But I . . ."

"If you don't come with me, I think you'll regret it. The young lady is invited also."

He kept his arm on my shoulder and led me around to the front of the club, with Penny beside me. He took us over to the big black car that I had seen pull up earlier. He opened the back door and said, "Tom Frost, this is Ed Sullivan."

And it was.

Really.

No lie.

Ed Sullivan *in person,* right there in front of me.

One of the most famous guys in the world, the host of a show I'd been watching on TV every Sunday night, was reaching out to shake my hand. He was littler than I thought, but he was still Ed Sullivan.

He was looking at me real serious. He sounded exactly like he did on TV.

"Joey Martino's chimp died today."

I didn't know what to say. Who was Joey Martino? How did his chimp die? Why was Ed Sullivan saying this to me?

"I'm . . . I'm sorry, Mr. Sullivan," I said.

"So was Joe. So was I. Best damn chimp act I'd seen in fifteen years. He was going to be on my show tomorrow night. Now I got a problem: my show is two minutes short. I need a new act. You have any ideas on who I should get?"

Why was he asking me? He was Ed Sullivan. He knew everybody in show business. He couldn't think of anybody to have on his show because some guy's chimp had died?

"I . . . I don't know who you should have on your show, sir," I said.

"What about you?"

He was kidding.

He *had* to be kidding.

Or maybe it was a guy who just looked and talked like Ed Sullivan and Penny had hired him to play a big joke on me. She was rich. She could've done that. There were plenty of comedians who did imitations of Ed Sullivan. I looked at him closer. Nobody looked *exactly* like Ed Sullivan and talked *exactly* like Ed Sullivan, and this guy did. He was Ed Sullivan and he wasn't joking.

"You want me on your show?" I asked.

"Yes."

"*Your* show?"

"Yes."

"*The Ed Sullivan Show?*"

He smiled for the first time. "I think that's what they call it."

Penny hugged me again. Number eight. She started screaming. "Oh my God! Oh my God!"

Ed Sullivan crossed his arms, just like he does on TV, and said, "There's nothing I enjoy more than giving someone their big break. I come downtown a lot to check out new acts and find performers that no one's seen before. Now, this folk music scene is big and you're fresh and new and I liked your song. Very powerful stuff. You got an agent or manager?"

I shook my head. "No, sir."

He looked over at the guy in the shiny suit who had dragged me over and kind of laughed and said, "Good!" Then he looked back at me and said, "Don't worry, son, we'll take care of you. Rehearsal tomorrow is at noon sharp. Show's at eight. Be on time and ready to go. Broadway and Fifty-third." He turned to the guy who had dragged me over. "Bob, give him some tickets."

The guy handed me six tickets to *The Ed Sullivan Show*.

"See you tomorrow," said Ed Sullivan. Then he closed the car door and drove away.

I felt like I was in a dream and a movie and a nightmare all at the same time. It *had* to be a dream. But it wasn't. It was really happening. I had to get out of there. I had to go home. I started walking down the street toward the subway station.

Penny ran after me. "Hey! Wait up!"

I was talking out loud to myself. "That was really Ed Sullivan. . . . I talked to Ed Sullivan. . . . Ed Sullivan talked to me." I looked at the tickets in my hand. "Ed Sullivan gave me tickets to his show." I gave three of them to Penny. "Here."

"You're gonna be on *Ed Sullivan* and sing my song!" she screamed.

I stopped walking and turned to her. "No, I'm not."

"He just asked you to!"

"He's crazy!" I said.

"He's not crazy! He's Ed Sullivan!"

"Penny, this is ridiculous! I don't *want* to be on *The Ed Sullivan Show*!"

She stared at me for a second and then she said, "Why'd you buy a guitar?"

"I told you why."

"Because you wanted to be a folksinger. Right?"

"Yeah."

"Well, now you are."

I took a deep breath. It was getting pretty cold. Every time we said something that smoke stuff came out of our mouths.

"Penny, I felt like I was gonna have a heart attack singing up there just now and that was only a hundred people. If I was on *Ed Sullivan* there would be millions of people—"

Penny grabbed my arm really hard. She was strong. "Tom, listen to me, this is the chance of a lifetime. People spend years trying to get on that show."

"That's because they *want* to be on it! I don't!"

"They'll pay you!"

"I don't care! I wouldn't do it for a million bucks!"

"Would you do it for me?"

Why did she have to say that? Now I felt even worse, like I was letting her down. It was awful. There we were having a big argument and ten minutes ago I was about to kiss her, and I would have if it hadn't been for that stupid Ed Sullivan!

"Penny, I can't do it."

"Yes, you can, Tom."

"How do you know?"

"Because . . . I think you can."

How could she possibly think somebody like me could do something like that? Even if I *did* go on the show, I knew it would be the worst disaster of all time.

"Tom, please, just *sing* the song. You have the chance to say something to millions of people. Think about that kid that got arrested. The song is about him. If you won't do it for me—"

"Penny—"

"—then do it for him. Tom, you can make a statement here. You can make a difference."

"Penny, one stupid song isn't going to make a difference in the world."

She crossed her arms and looked really mad. "Oh? So the song is stupid?"

"No, I didn't mean that. What I meant is I'm not gonna change anybody's mind."

"How do you know? You can at least try! Tom, you could do something really important!"

"But I don't want to do anything important!"

"*I* do!"

"Then *you* do it!"

"Ed Sullivan didn't ask me! He asked you!"

We were really yelling at each other. We sounded like Jackie Gleason and his wife on *The Honeymooners*. People were looking at us.

"Penny, I gotta go home."

She just stared at me.

"So, why'd you do it, Tom? Why'd you do all this?"

"I told you. . . ."

"To meet a girl? To find some chick that'd make out with you? Maybe cop a feel? And maybe, if you're *really* lucky, she'd let you go all the way, right?"

"That's not true."

"Liar!"

She was right. It was true. I mean, I had wanted all that, except it was different now. But I knew I couldn't sing her song on *The Ed Sullivan Show*. And I knew I'd never see her again when I told her.

"Penny, I can't. . . . I'm sorry. I'm just not the kind of person that can do important stuff like that. I wish I was . . . but I'm not."

Her eyes were all red and it looked like she was going to cry, but I could tell she was mad. "You know, I may hate almost everything my father stands for, but at least he has the courage to get up and say what he thinks."

"Penny, I'm—"

"Goodbye."

She started to walk away.

"Penny, wait."

"I hate that name!" She started walking faster.

I ran after her. "Where are you going?"

"None of your damn business!"

I grabbed her arm. She turned and looked at me like no one's ever looked at me before. Then she said, "Let go of me, you creep."

I let go of her arm.

She walked away and disappeared around the corner.

She was gone.

I stood there for a minute. After a while I noticed this guy was standing across the street looking at me. He crossed the street and came up to me and said, "Excuse me? Can I have your autograph?"

"What?"

He held out a piece of paper and a pen. "Can I have your autograph?"

"What for?"

"You just sang at Folk Town. You're somebody, aren't you?"

I shook my head. "No. I'm nobody."

THE LAST THING
I WANTED TO DO

I just started walking. I didn't care where I was going. I didn't care if my parents woke up and found out I wasn't home and I got in trouble. I didn't care about anything. I walked through some pretty scary places, but I wasn't even that scared. I ended up by the river. As soon as I saw it, I knew what I had to do.

I took my guitar case and threw it as hard as I could into the river. It was pretty dark and hard to see, but I saw it land and make a little splash. I watched it float on top of the water for a while and waited for it to sink, but it didn't. I wondered if it would just float like that forever. I wondered if it would float out to the ocean, or maybe it would wash ashore and some kid would find it and get all excited. Of course the water would probably wreck the guitar and it would get all warped. Finally it started to sink and down it went. It looked like a little ship sinking. As soon as it was gone, I walked back to the subway. I finally got home and the sun was almost up and I snuck back into the house. I didn't even change out of my folksinger clothes. I just got in my bed and closed my eyes. I'd never felt so tired in my life.

"Morning, Tommy!" said my mom, poking her head in my door. "Time for church."

I had only been asleep for about forty-five minutes. When I woke up I felt okay for about two seconds and then I remembered what happened with Penny and I felt horrible again. I took a shower and got dressed in my nice clothes, ate breakfast, and went to church. I almost fell asleep about six times. It was another boring sermon and our minister had this voice that always put you to sleep, even when you weren't tired. On the way home in the car, sitting in the backseat, I did finally pass out.

"Wake up, champ!" yelled my father. "We got hydrangeas waiting for us!"

As soon as we got home I had to change into my work clothes and help my father. It was freezing cold outside and we were cutting and pulling out hydrangeas for hours. Even though it was about thirty below I was sweating like crazy and getting all scratched up on the stupid bushes. We had to stack them in these stupid little piles and tie them up so the trashmen would take them. My father tied up most of them because, as usual, he said I wasn't doing it right, so mostly I just stood there and froze and watched him. I was so tired I could hardly keep my eyes open.

"Can we take a break?" I asked.

"We'll take a break when we're finished," said my father.

Finally, after about a hundred hours of torture, we finished. I took another shower because I was all sweaty and dirty and then I just fell on top of my bed. I'd never been so tired in all my life. All I wanted to do was sleep for a week. Just as I was kind of falling asleep, I heard my mom come in and pick up my dirty clothes to do the wash.

Two minutes later my mom and my father were standing over my bed.

"Tom!" yelled my father.

I woke up and they were staring down at me.

"Do you have something to tell us, young man?" asked my father.

They had found out.

They knew I had snuck out.

They were going to kill me.

"About what?" I asked.

"About yesterday," said my mother.

I propped myself up on my elbow and tried to look real nonchalant. "What about yesterday?"

"You did something," said my father.

"Did what?" I asked.

My mother held her hand up and she was holding the tickets. "You got three tickets to *The Ed Sullivan Show!* I was doing

138

your laundry and I found them in your pants! To think I almost ruined them!"

"Where'd you get these?" asked my father.

Phew.

I wasn't going to get killed.

But I had to think pretty fast.

I did a fake yawn and then I said, "Uh, this guy was handing them out near the place I got my guitar. I forgot to tell you."

"How could you forget something like that?" asked my mom. "Oh, I'm so excited I can hardly stand it!"

"Calm down, Louise," said my father, and then he pointed at me. "Get dressed. It says on the ticket we have to be there by six o'clock."

The last thing I wanted to do was go to see *The Ed Sullivan Show*. What if someone saw me? What if Ed Sullivan saw me and yelled at me because I didn't show up? I tried to make myself look as sick as I could.

"I . . . I don't feel very well. I don't think I should go."

My mom put her hand on my forehead. "You don't feel hot."

My father leaned over the bed. "This is *The Ed Sullivan Show*. If I have to put you in a wheelchair, you're going! This is something you can tell your grandchildren!"

We all got dressed up in the same exact clothes we had worn to church that morning. Before we left my father said we all had to go to the bathroom at our house. He didn't want any of us to have to use a bathroom in New York. I kept saying I was sick and my father kept saying I had to go. I finally figured that since I was just going to be sitting in the audience, Ed Sullivan wasn't going to see me. And if he did see me, I'd be in my church clothes and wearing glasses and I'd look completely different from the folksinger guy he wanted on his show.

We drove into Manhattan. My mom gave me some aspirin and made me lie down in the backseat. My father was in a pretty good mood for a change. I could tell he was just as excited as my mom was, but he was trying not to show it.

"Oh, I hope Topo Gigio will be on the show," said my mom. Topo Gigio was this little mouse puppet that was on the show a lot and Ed Sullivan would talk to him and Topo Gigio would always make Ed Sullivan kiss him. My mom was crazy about Topo Gigio.

I was wondering who they were going to put on instead of me. There were probably a million jugglers and comedians and singers and dancers in New York that Ed Sullivan could call up. Or maybe there was some famous person who was in New York and Ed would call them. I could easily imagine him calling up somebody like Frank Sinatra and saying, "Frankie? This is Ed. Can you come down and do a song on the show tonight? Some creep kid folksinger didn't show up!"

And Frank Sinatra would say, "What a lousy, ungrateful punk! No problem, Ed, I'll be there!"

We parked the car and my father complained about how much he had to pay for parking, as usual. We got in a big line in front of the theater to wait to go in. There were all kinds of different people in line: old people, people like my parents, a couple of nuns, some sailors, and even some kids. There were

140

even some pretty women who looked like secretaries, but I didn't pay that much attention to them. Up on a big sign in front of the theater, they had the names of some of the people who were going to be on the show. In a way I was really glad that it didn't say Tom Frost up there and in a way I kind of wished it did.

We finally went inside and sat down in our seats. We were pretty close to the front. I hoped we weren't so close that Ed Sullivan or that guy in the shiny suit who gave me the tickets would see me. There were all these people running around the stage getting ready, moving cameras and turning on lights.

"This is so exciting!" said my mom for the millionth time.

My father was looking around, trying to act like a big shot. "It's so small. I thought it would be a really big place. You know what I mean?" And then he did the worst impression of Ed Sullivan I have ever heard. "I thought it would be a really big shew!" That's what Ed Sullivan said all the time. My father laughed and my mom laughed. They were having a really good time. I felt miserable.

A guy came out onstage and told everybody what to do during the commercials and when to clap and when to laugh.

My father crossed his arms and said, "I'm only going to laugh if something's funny."

I was looking at the stage and wondering what it would have been like to actually get up there and sing the song. I had to admit it would've been pretty exciting and maybe even fun in a scary kind of way. Like the first time I rode the Cyclone at Coney Island. It was scary as hell at first, but afterward I felt really cool that I had done it. On the other hand, it was a big relief to sit there and know I wasn't going to have to sing a song in front of millions of people. But then I started to feel lousy again because I let Penny down and now she hated my guts. I knew I'd never see her again, so it didn't matter, but I *wanted* to see her again because I really liked her and she was the only girl that had ever liked me at all. Plus she was pretty and funny and smart and she could do all that cool stuff like get a taxi really fast and make a harmonica holder out of a coat hanger; and she actually thought I could've gotten up there and done something important. And now she was gone. I slouched down in my seat.

"Tom, sit up!" said my father.

I sat up.

And that's when I saw her.

I couldn't believe it.

Penny and her parents were coming down the aisle and they were going to sit right next to us.

GOING TO RUSSIA

I had completely forgotten that she had the other three tickets, and even if I had remembered, I wouldn't have thought she would use them. But her parents probably reacted exactly the same way my parents reacted because *The Ed Sullivan Show* was a big deal.

Penny saw me and saw that she was going to have to sit next to me. She turned to her mother and said, "You go in first."

Her mother said, "No. I get claustrophobic. I want the aisle."

Penny sat down right next to me. I just stared straight ahead at the stage and didn't say anything. My mom got all excited because I was sitting next to a girl, and she leaned over and whispered in my ear, "Talk to that girl."

"No," I said.

"At least say hello."

"No."

"Introduce yourself."

"No!"

I know Penny heard every word my mother was saying. My mother was a lousy whisperer; she was the worst whisperer in the world. I *really* wanted the show to start.

All of a sudden Penny turned to me and said, "Hi. My name's Penny. What's yours?" She said it real fake. I could tell she was still really mad at me. My mom got all smiley. I didn't say anything. My mom jabbed me in my ribs with her elbow, really hard, so I would say something.

I turned to Penny and said, "My name's Tom."

"Tom, that's a nice name. Aren't you excited to be seeing *The Ed Sullivan Show?*" She was still being really fake. She wasn't even talking in her normal voice. "I bet it's even more exciting when you're actually *on* the show. Think how exciting that must be! Gosh, that must be the most exciting thing ever!"

Of course, my mom was going crazy because this really pretty girl was talking to me, and I was going crazy because I knew Penny wanted to kill me and because her father kept looking over at me.

Finally, after about a million years, the show started. The same guy who told everybody to laugh came out and told everybody to clap like crazy when Ed Sullivan came out. The orchestra started playing and all the lights came on. My mom grabbed my father's hand because she was so excited. I couldn't remember ever seeing them holding hands.

This big voice came over the speakers. "Good evening, ladies and gentlemen! Tonight from New York, *The Ed Sullivan Show*! And now, live from New York, Ed Sullivan!"

Ed Sullivan came out and stood in front of that little curtain he always stands in front of. He didn't look as short as he did when I met him in front of Folk Town.

"Good evening, ladies and gentlemen. Tonight we have some wonderful performers for you. The great pianist, direct from London, Liberace. From Greece, the Fabulous Korkis Jugglers. A delightful scene from the hit Broadway musical *Oliver!*, tap dancer Peg Leg Bates, the very funny comedian Jackie . . ."

All of a sudden Penny leaned over and whispered in my ear, "Aren't you glad you don't have to sing that stupid song tonight?"

"Penny, it wasn't your song—"

Penny's father leaned over and gave me a really dirty look and went, "Shhh!"

Ed Sullivan kept talking. ". . . and the great actor Mr. Orson Welles. We'll be right back after a word from Lincoln Continental!"

We all clapped like we were supposed to, and then a guy yelled, "Sixty seconds for commercial!"

I turned to Penny and said, "Look, I didn't mean your song was—"

She said, "Excuse me," and stood up and started to walk toward the aisle.

Her father got all mad. "The show just started! Where are you going?"

"To Russia," she said.

"Don't get sassy with me, young lady!"

"I have to go to the bathroom."

"What for?" he asked.

"Two guesses."

She walked out our row and up the aisle. I had to talk to her, so I told my parents I had to go to the bathroom, too.

Now *my* father got all mad. "I told you to go at home!"

"I did."

"So why do you have to go again?"

"I don't know."

The big voice came over the loudspeaker. "We are coming back! Get ready to applaud. Five, four . . ."

My father pushed me back in my seat. "You can't go now. They're about to start! Sit down!"

"I gotta go!"

"Hold it!"

"I can't!"

"Yes, you can!"

Even though both my father and I were whispering all this stuff, and we were both much better whisperers than my mom, she was getting embarrassed. "Let him go, Harold!"

My father is really strong and he was holding my arm so I couldn't move. I had to think of something fast. I put my hand up to my mouth and said, "I think I'm gonna throw up."

146

I don't think my father liked the idea of me possibly throwing up all over everybody, so he let go of me pretty fast. I walked up the aisle and asked the usher where the bathrooms were. He said I couldn't come back in until the next commercial break, but I didn't care.

Penny was just about to go into the women's restroom when I caught up with her. I was glad she hadn't gone in because I would have had to wait outside or maybe even go in after her. The only time I had been in a women's restroom was in elementary school when I was in second grade and Elliot Freeman dared me to go in. It wasn't that big of a deal once I saw it.

"Penny, wait a minute!"

She started to go into the bathroom but I grabbed her. She crossed her arms and gave me a really dirty look. "What do you want?"

"I'm sorry I said that about your song. It's not a stupid song."

"I *know* it's not a stupid song. I'm the one who was stupid for thinking you'd sing it."

"I wanted to sing it for you. Really. I did. I wish I could have, but . . ."

"Well, it's too late now."

"Yeah, I know."

She let out one of those sighs people do when they're really frustrated. "You know, you're just as bad as that cop who arrested that kid."

That made me kind of mad. "What are you talking about?"

"He arrested that guy just because he was a negro, even

though he didn't steal your guitar, and you didn't do anything to stop him."

"What was I supposed to do? I told him it wasn't the guy! He wouldn't listen to me!"

"You could have told somebody else what happened."

"Who? Who's going to listen to me?"

"About twenty million people could have been listening tonight."

She had me there.

"Tom, what happened to that kid is what the whole song is about. Did you even hear what you were singing?"

"Yeah. Of course I did."

To be honest, at first I hadn't thought about the words that much. I was just trying to memorize the song. But the more I had thought about that cop and the kid, and since I had seen it right in front of me, not like on TV or reading about it in a newspaper, the whole song seemed different. Penny was right. But still, the idea of me singing the song on *The Ed Sullivan Show* was a whole different matter.

"I guess you should've found yourself a real folksinger."

"Yeah. I guess I should have. Look, I really do have to use the restroom."

I was standing in front of the door, so I moved out of the way. "Sorry."

She started to go in, but then she stopped and said, "You should quit shortchanging yourself on what you think you can do and you can't do."

I nodded.

"Goodbye, Tom."

ED SULLIVAN'S NEPHEW

The way she had said "goodbye" was worse than if she had said "I hate you."

I started to walk back to my seat and my mind was going like a million miles an hour. Then it got really weird. All the stuff that Penny had been saying started to get to me. I put my hand on the door that went to where the audience was and all of a sudden I froze. I thought if I went through that door I would know exactly what was going to happen to me for the rest of my life. It was like I was watching a movie of myself. I'd go back to my seat and watch the show and then I'd go home with my parents and go to school the next day and everything would be just like it always was. Nothing would change. I'd be a creep, Penny would never see me again, I'd keep thinking about that kid, and for the rest of my life I'd be wondering what would have happened if I had sung on *The Ed Sullivan Show.*

I guess that's what made me do what I did.

I walked past the bathrooms and around a corner where there was a guard in a uniform standing in front of a door with a sign that said NO ADMITTANCE WHEN RED LIGHT IS ON.

I tried to talk in a real deep, important voice. "Excuse me, I need to get backstage."

The guard said, "You can't go in here, kid. Go back in the audience."

"But I need to get backstage and talk to Mr. Sullivan."

The guard smiled. "Yeah, yeah, yeah. And I need to do my job. Now turn around and go back in and sit down."

My voice went up a little higher. It always does that when I get nervous. I hate it. I sound like Alvin from The Chipmunks. "Sir, I *have* to get backstage."

"Well, you can't get backstage unless you got a pass or I got your name on the list." He tapped his pencil on a piece of paper that he had on a clipboard. I thought for a second that my name might be on the list because I *was* supposed to be in the show.

"My name's Tom Frost."

He looked down at the list. "Your name's on the list . . ."

I started to walk in, but he put out his arm and stopped me.

". . . but it's crossed out." He showed me the list. They must have crossed it out when I missed the rehearsal. I knew he wasn't going to let me in so I walked away and around the corner. I had to figure another way to get in. Maybe there was another door?

As I went down the hall, this delivery guy came running down the hallway with the biggest bunch of flowers I had ever seen in my life. It was as big as a TV set. All you could see were the delivery guy's legs because the flowers blocked the whole rest of his body. He was holding a box of candy, too.

"Hey, kid," he said. "Do you know where the backstage entrance is?"

I started to point and then I got an idea. "Uh . . . who is it for?"

"Orson Welles."

Orson Welles was one of the guys that was going to be on the show. I had never heard of him, but my father told me he was an actor and I figured he had to be pretty famous to be on *The Ed Sullivan Show.*

I reached out for the flowers and candy. "I'll take it in for you."

"Nothing doing, kid."

"Really, it's no trouble at all." I sounded so fake when I said that. I even did this stupid English accent, don't ask me why. "I do stuff like this all the time."

"You work here?" he asked, real suspicious.

"Yes, I do. I work here."

"Aren't you kinda young?"

I took a deep breath and looked him right in the eye. "My name is Tom Sullivan. I'm Ed Sullivan's nephew. Would you like to ask Uncle Ed if I'm too young to work here?"

Now, I don't know whether he really bought it, or he just wanted to go home, or he was in a hurry and had to go make some other delivery, but he said, "You make sure these get to Orson Welles or I'll come back and give you a knuckle sandwich."

"Don't worry," I said. "He'll get them."

"Good. And say hi to Uncle Ed for me."

He gave me the flowers and candy and walked away. The flowers were a lot heavier than I thought they'd be. I held them way up in front of my face, so you couldn't see me, and walked back toward the security guard. I tried to make my voice sound like the delivery guy's. "Flowers and candy for Mr. Orson Welles."

The guard looked down at the list and said, "Dressing room number four."

I wasn't completely sure what I was going to do once I got backstage. But even if they threw me out, at least I'd know that I had *tried* to do something, and maybe Penny would even see me getting thrown out. It was pretty crowded backstage, all these people were running around, but everybody was real quiet because the show was going on. I kept the flowers in front of my face and looked through them and I could see right onto the stage. There were a bunch of jugglers throwing wine bottles and torches and a guitar around.

This really pretty woman with glasses came up to me and whispered, "Can I help you?"

"Where's dressing room four?" I asked.

She pointed down a hallway and I walked off. I figured I would deliver the flowers to the old movie star guy but hold on to the candy box. That way I could keep wandering around, and if someone asked me what I was doing, I could say I was delivering candy to somebody else. I stuffed the candy box down the front of my pants and hid it under my jacket.

I walked past another pretty woman in a low-cut dress who was really stacked. She asked, "'Ello? Those flowers for me, luv?" I think she was from England from the way she talked, or maybe she was just pretending to be.

I said, "No, ma'am. Sorry."

I finally found dressing room number four. I knocked on the door and this big booming voice said, "Open, locks, who-ever knocks!"

I opened the door and there was a big tall guy with a beard sitting in front of a mirror. A really pretty girl was putting makeup on him. It seemed like every girl in the place was pretty.

"Are you Orson Welles?" I asked.

"I damn well better be!" he said, and then he laughed. The makeup girl laughed, too.

My father had told me that Orson Welles used to be a famous movie star and director and had been married to Rita Hayworth, who I guess was some big sexpot, but then he got fat. I kind of felt sorry for him, but not too much. I mean, there he was on *The Ed Sullivan Show* and a pretty girl was leaning over him, combing his hair.

I held up the flowers. "Uh, these are for you, sir."

"You are mistaken, young man," he said. "These are not for me." Then he turned to the makeup girl, held the flowers out to her, and started reciting a poem in this really dramatic voice.

> I would I had some flowers o' the spring that might
> Become your time of day; and yours, and yours,
> That wear upon your virgin branches yet
> Your maidenheads growing.

I didn't know what he was talking about, but the girl started giggling when he said "virgin branches." Then he nodded to a skinny guy who was sitting on a sofa and pointed at me. "Leonard, this young gentleman deserves a tip for his splendid services. I believe twenty dollars would suffice."

I couldn't believe it.

The skinny guy gave me twenty bucks. I had never gotten that much money at one time. Even at Christmas, the most I ever got was ten dollars from my aunt Evy, the one who smoked. That delivery guy would be really mad if he knew he missed a twenty-dollar tip.

"Thank you, sir," I said. "Thank you very much!"

"Now go away!" he bellowed.

SOMETHING REALLY
BIG AND AWFUL

I went out the door and pulled the candy out from under my jacket. The box kind of got squished a little, but it still looked okay. In the hallway there were these little tiny speakers on the walls and I could hear Ed Sullivan's voice coming out of them saying, "C'mon, let's hear it for the Fabulous Korkis Jugglers!"

I had to find some different clothes. I figured they had to have a costume place somewhere and I asked *another* pretty woman where it was and she told me. It was kind of hard to find, and the whole time I was looking for it I kept thinking that I was going to get thrown out of there. I recognized Orson Welles's voice coming out of the little speakers in the hallway.

It sounded like he was reciting a poem by somebody like Shakespeare or something.

I finally found a door that said WARDROBE on it. I knew that "wardrobe" meant costumes from when I was in a play they made us do in sixth grade. Miss Pippin, the lousy-looking teacher with the sexy legs, made us call our clothes wardrobe instead of costumes. Don't ask me why. Anyway, the stupid door was locked and I was trying to think of what I was going to do when all of a sudden this guy yelled at me, "Outta the way, moron!"

He was pushing a big thing on wheels and he practically ran me over with it. I was pretty mad until I saw it was a big rack of costumes. He tried to open the door, but he didn't have a key, and he said some really bad swearwords and then he stomped away. But he left all those costumes right there in front of me. All I needed was something to cover up my jacket and a hat and a pair of dark glasses so nobody would recognize me. I found a big sweater and put it on over my jacket. It was kind of warm, but it covered everything up pretty well. I found a little brown cap. It wasn't like the one I had bought yesterday, but it kind of looked like something a folksinger would wear. I put it on and headed toward the stage.

I saw this greasy-looking guy in the hallway, leaning against the wall. He had a pair of sunglasses on top of his head, the way cool people wear them when they're inside someplace.

"Could I borrow your sunglasses for about ten minutes?" I asked.

"*Borrow* my sunglasses? No friggin' way," he said.

I held up the box of candy. "You can have this candy?"

He gave me this real disgusted look. "*Candy?* What am I? A little kid? I don't want your friggin' candy. Hey? Who are you? Are you supposed to be back here?"

I had to do something drastic. "I'll give you twenty bucks for your sunglasses."

He didn't look so disgusted anymore. "*Twenty* bucks?"

"Yeah."

"Deal!"

I gave him the money. He gave me the sunglasses and I put them on. They were really cruddy. They probably cost the guy like two bucks, but I had to have them.

I went back to the side of the stage and I could see there was a comedian on, but nobody in the audience was laughing at him. I saw Ed Sullivan standing off to the side watching the comedian. I didn't know whether he'd kill me or throw me out of the place or both, but I had to try. I walked up to him and I could hear him whispering to another man, "This guy stinks! How could he be funny at the rehearsal and now he's bombing?"

It was probably the worst time to talk to him, but I had to. "Excuse me? Mr. Sullivan?"

He whipped around and glared at me. He was a little guy, but he was really scary.

"Who are you?"

"I'm Tom Frost. The folksinger."

He was whispering, but he got *really* mad. "You son of a bitch! Where the hell were you? You missed the rehearsal!"

"I'm sorry, sir."

"What do you think you're doing coming here? Where's security?" He started to look around for a guard.

"Sir, I just wanted to tell you that I couldn't come because . . ."

I had to think of something really big and really awful.

". . . my mother died today."

I couldn't believe I'd said that. But it had to be something really bad and that was the worst thing I could think of.

"She was real sick and she wanted to see me on your show, but I couldn't leave her because, you know, she was dying . . . and she died . . . and . . . and . . . it was her birthday."

Ed Sullivan stared at me for a second like he was going to rip my head off. Then all of a sudden he laughed.

"Kid, I don't believe a word you said. But you got balls!"

I couldn't believe he said that. He grabbed my arm and spun me around toward a guy wearing headphones. "Put this kid on next and pull off that lousy comedian!"

I almost fainted.

"Where's your guitar?" he asked.

I am so stupid.

I had *completely* forgotten about my guitar.

"It . . . it . . . got stolen," I said. This was actually the truth. Of course I had gotten it back and thrown it in the river, but I wasn't going to tell that to Ed Sullivan.

"Get a guitar from the orchestra!" he told the guy standing next to him.

"We don't have time!" said the guy who was wearing headphones.

I remembered seeing a guitar.

"Those jugglers had one," I said. "Could I use theirs?"

One guy ran over to the jugglers and grabbed their guitar. Another guy grabbed my arm and led me to the side of the stage. They gave me the guitar and pushed me over to right behind the curtain that the comedian guy was standing in front of telling his jokes. They lowered a microphone on a really long pole over my head.

The comedian guy was telling another lousy joke and no one was laughing and all of a sudden the orchestra started playing music and he got all confused and then he stopped talking. The spotlight on him went out and a guy dragged him off and he was *really* mad. He said something even worse than the costume guy.

They raised the curtain in front of me and all I could see were bright lights. Then I heard Ed Sullivan on the other side of the stage. "And now, ladies and gentlemen, we have a little surprise for you. Last night my wife, Sylvia, and I were at one of those charming little Greenwich Village coffeehouses downtown and we spotted a talented folksinger who was playing the folk music that is so popular with the youngsters these days. I wanted to bring him here tonight to sing for you, and so let's hear it for Tom Frost!"

I really hoped Penny was watching this.

THE GREATEST SMILE
OF ALL TIME

It was a lot scarier than the Cyclone at Coney Island and a gazillion times worse than singing at Folk Town.

The sweater was making me really hot with all the clothes I had on under it, so I was sweating like crazy. My knees were shaking and I had a giant pounding headache, like in those corny TV commercials where there's a little guy inside your head and he's hitting your brain with a big hammer.

I looked down at the guitar. There were no red dots, but I remembered where to put my fingers. I didn't have a pick, so I just strummed with my thumb. I also didn't have the paper that Penny had written the words to the song down on. What if I couldn't remember all the words?

I opened my mouth to sing. My mouth was completely dry. I couldn't make a sound. I swallowed and that was better.

I started to sing.

I know this sounds really weird, but it didn't even feel like I was singing the song. It felt like the song was singing me.

America is the land of the free,
That's what my teachers always taught me
To be an American is to be lucky
Because all Americans are free
But it don't look that way to me,
Take a look around and what do you see?

That's an American sitting in the back of the bus
That's an American going to a different school
*   than us*
That's an American sitting way up in the balcony
That's an American has to use a different door
*   than you and me*
That's an American drinking from a different
*   water fountain*
That's an American whose vote nobody's countin'
That's an American who can't move in
To some neighborhood 'cause of the color of his
*   skin*
That's an American being beaten by a cop
Knocked down by a fire hose so he can't get up
That's an American hanging from a tree
That's an American who's supposed to be free

Take a look around and what do you see?
Lot of Americans and they ain't free
Who said America's the land of the free?
It don't look that way to me.

I finished playing the song. The people in the audience started clapping. I knew most of them were clapping because the sign was telling them to, but I hoped some of them were clapping because they liked Penny's song.

Ed Sullivan waved his hand for me to come over. I stood next to him and he turned to the audience and said, "I just want to wish this young man success and a long career. Now, c'mon, let's hear it for him!" The audience clapped again and then he said, "That's our show for tonight. We'll see you next week, when our guests will be the great Kate Smith, the U.S. Naval Academy Marching Band, silent film star Buster Keaton, ballet dancers Rudolf Nureyev and Margot Fonteyn, comedian Jose Jimenez, and my little friend Topo Gigio! Good night!"

I ran off the stage as fast as I could past all these people who were saying things to me and trying to shake my hand. I gave the juggling guy his guitar back and I tore off the sweater and took off the hat and tossed them on the wardrobe rack. I kept the sunglasses. I wasn't going to throw them away after paying twenty bucks. I went out the door, past the security guard, and ran into the restroom. I was still sweating like crazy so I wiped my face off with some paper towels.

I couldn't believe I had just sung on *The Ed Sullivan Show*.

I wondered who had been watching. I wondered if those girls from my school, Connie and Jeannie, had seen it. And Mr. Liotta, who yelled at me for raising the flag; and that model and the photographer who hated folksingers; and Joey Martino, the guy whose chimpanzee had died; and all those Japanese tourists; and Max, the guy who taught me how to play E minor; and those folkie guys from Washington Square; and that mime guy at Folk Town; and even the cop who had arrested that kid. I knew one song wouldn't change a guy like that, but it might change some other person's mind or maybe some kid who was watching it would think about it and wouldn't grow up to be like that cop.

I came out of the restroom just as my parents were coming out of the theater and right toward me. I was looking for Penny, but I didn't see her.

"Where the hell have you been?" asked my father. "You missed the whole damn show!"

I tried to look sick. "I . . . I didn't feel good. I was in the bathroom."

My father looked at me real suspicious. "I *checked* the bathroom. Your mother made me look for you."

"Uh, I went outside for a little bit to get some fresh air," I said. "You must have just missed me."

My mom put her hand on my forehead. "Oh, honey, you're hot and you're sweating. Harold, he's sick, we shouldn't have made him come."

"It's okay, Mom, I feel better now. How was the show?"

"It was wonderful!" said my mom. "I *loved* Liberace!"

My father made a face and then he said, "Those jugglers were pretty good."

I was still looking around for Penny. My mom put her hand on my forehead again.

"Mom, don't!"

She took her hand off and said, "I'm so sorry you missed the show, there was one of those folksingers I bet you would have enjoyed."

"Oh, yeah?" I asked. "Was he good?"

My father laughed. "He was a folksinger!"

"*I* liked him very much," said my mom. "He reminded me of you, Tommy."

My heart stopped.

Did she know?

"I bet if you keep practicing your guitar, you could do something like that someday."

"Over my dead body," said my father.

"Oh, Harold, you'd be so proud to have Tom sing on *The Ed Sullivan Show*. What parent wouldn't?"

She winked at me.

She knew.

Or did she?

My father took her arm. "C'mon, we gotta get out of here before the traffic starts up."

I saw Penny coming toward us, talking to her parents.

"I've gotta go to the restroom," she said to her father. "I'll meet you outside."

"Make it snappy!" said her father as he dragged Penny's mother outside.

I looked over at Penny and saw her smiling at me. It looked like she wanted to run over and hug me again, but I knew she wouldn't because my parents were right there. I turned to them and said, "I'll meet you guys at the car."

My father started to get mad. "Meet us at the car? What are you talking about?"

"I gotta talk to that girl for a minute."

My mother looked at me like I had just given her a million dollars. My father started to say something, but my mother grabbed him and practically dragged him outside.

Penny walked over to me. She was pretending like it was no big deal, acting like nothing had happened, but I could tell she was really happy. She stuck her hands in her coat pockets and said, "Too bad you missed the show."

"Was it good?" I asked.

"Yeah. It was."

"What was your favorite act?"

She pretended to think for a little bit and then said, "The folksinger."

"Yeah? I heard he sang a really great song."

She nodded. "He did."

"So, you liked him?"

She smiled the greatest smile of all time. "I loved him."

WHATEVER HAPPENED
TO TOM FROST?

The next day at school a lot of people were talking about the folksinger who was on *The Ed Sullivan Show*. A few days later there was an article in the *New York Times* about how he had disappeared and nobody could find him. The headline said "Where Is Tom Frost?" Supposedly Ed Sullivan paid detectives to look for him and some big-time show business agents were trying to find him so they could be his agents and sign him to a record contract and put him in the movies and all sorts of crazy stuff.

I didn't say anything to anybody.

I'd gone about as far as a kid with one chord could go.

Tom Frost had retired.

*   *   *

The next weekend, Penny and I tried to find out what happened to that kid who got arrested for stealing my guitar. We went down to a police station near where the cop gave me my guitar back. The police said they didn't know anything about him. So we went to another station in the Village and got the same story. Penny said we'd keep trying, so I guess that's what we're gonna do next weekend.

Penny went with me to the Tom Turkey Dance. They changed the name and called it the Snow Ball, since Thanksgiving was over and it was practically Christmas. The gym was all decorated with balloons and streamers and they turned down the lights, but it still looked like a gym. They had a dance band at one end, playing underneath one of the basketball hoops. It was the kind of band that plays at weddings, with guys in suits playing saxophoes and trumpets and clarinets, and they all sat down behind those little stands with the name of the band painted on them. They were called the Young Tones, but none of them were young. Mr. Liotta was walking around making sure nobody was spiking the punch or dancing too close or making out.

Penny and I were dancing in the corner of the gym, right next to that stupid rope they make you climb in P.E. Neither of us was very good at dancing. We just kind of rocked back and forth a lot. But that's basically what everybody else was doing, too, except George Gruber and his girlfriend, Nancy Marks, who were really good dancers. They did all those fancy moves and stuff and he was swinging her all over the place. They were kind of show-offs, but, I have to admit, if I could dance like that I'd probably be a show-off, too.

Penny had her head on my shoulder and the band was playing this song called "Blue Velvet."

"I hate this song," she said.

"Me too."

To be honest, I didn't really hate it, because even though it's a pretty corny song, it's a slow song and I had my arms around Penny and she smelled great and we were just rocking back and forth. I looked around the gym and saw Connie Brand and her big bosoms dancing with her boyfriend, Doug. He was a lousy dancer. He didn't look like he was having a good time at all. It looked like all he wanted to do was get out of there and get Connie in his Corvette. Jeannie Thomas was there, too, dancing with Tim, the pole-vaulter guy with the muscles. He looked even more bored than Doug did. Both Jeannie and Connie were all dressed up and they had a ton of makeup on and their hair was going way up high, but it was weird, they didn't look as pretty as they used to.

Penny lifted her head off my shoulder and looked up at me. "Do you wish people knew that you were Tom Frost?"

"Nobody'd believe it."

"I would."

She put her head back on my shoulder. We kept rocking back and forth for a little while and then she said, "You know, I was just thinking, it's too bad Tom Frost had to disappear."

"What do you mean?"

"Well, y'know, I have a lot of other poems."

"Penny—"

"We could do another song."

"I'm not—"

"I just finished that one about President Kennedy—"

"No!"

"We could call up Ed Sullivan . . ."

"NO!"

"But you could—"

I had to kiss her so she would stop talking. I guess that was our first official kiss. It was a pretty good one. But then Mr. Liotta came up and told us there was no kissing on the dance floor. Penny started arguing with him and we kind of got kicked out of the dance. I didn't care. It was pretty funny actually.

We ended up at a little diner. We just sat and talked and ate about a million French fries. I even had some coffee. It wasn't so bad when you put a ton of milk and sugar in it. They had a jukebox and Penny got all excited because it had a record by this new group she had told me about from England. She played the song six times in a row until the guy behind the counter unplugged the jukebox. It was a pretty cool song. Penny had given me her brother's guitar and I was taking lessons at Grayson's Music. Maybe the guitar teacher could teach that song to me? I hope it doesn't have too many chords.

I'm really glad I didn't jump off the George Washington Bridge.

Acknowledgments

If it wasn't for Lauri Hornik, this book would only be three chapters long and still hidden in my garage.

A good editor makes your book better; a great editor does so much more. Nancy Siscoe is a great editor.

Thanks to my agent, Richard Abate at ICM, and all the librarians who were nice to me.

DATE DUE

GAYLORD

PRINTED IN U.S.A.